"Samantha," Mrs. Jarvis said, a pleading note in her voice, "we've come to ask you to let us buy Shining—for Mandy."

For several long moments Samantha sat there, dumbfounded and unable to speak. Sell Shining? How could they ask her such a thing? How could she sell the first horse she'd ever owned? It had never crossed her mind. And to sell Shining now, when she finally seemed ready to race again?

"Um, I don't know," she muttered, scrambling to get her thoughts in order.

"We know how special Shining is to you," Mrs. Jarvis said quickly. "We know it's a lot to ask."

"It's just that we feel so strongly that Shining is the key to Mandy's complete recovery. She's formed a bond with the horse."

Samantha heaved a sigh. "I'll really have to think about it. I just don't know what to say right now."

Could she really consider giving up her own beautiful horse? What if she did, and Shining never had the opportunity to race? She was just beginning to show such promise.

Don't miss these exciting books from
HarperPaperbacks!

Collect all the books in the
THOROUGHBRED series:

#1 A Horse Called Wonder
#2 Wonder's Promise
#3 Wonder's First Race
#4 Wonder's Victory
#5 Ashleigh's Dream
#6 Wonder's Yearling
#7 Samantha's Pride
#8 Sierra's Steeplechase
#9 Pride's Challenge
#10 Pride's Last Race
#11 Wonder's Sister

Also by Joanna Campbell:

Battlecry Forever!
Star of Shadowbrook Farm

And look for

The Palomino
Christmas Colt
The Forgotten Filly
The Dream Horse

THOROUGHBRED

WONDER'S SISTER

JOANNA CAMPBELL

HarperPaperbacks

A Division of HarperCollins*Publishers*

This is a work of fiction. The characters, incidents, and dialogues are products of the author's imagination and are not to be construed as real. Any resemblance to actual events or persons, living or dead, is entirely coincidental.

 HarperPaperbacks   *A Division of* HarperCollins*Publishers*
10 East 53rd Street, New York, N.Y. 10022

Copyright © 1994 by Daniel Weiss Associates, Inc.,
and Joanna Campbell
Cover art copyright © 1994 Daniel Weiss Associates, Inc.

Produced by Daniel Weiss Associates, Inc., 33 West 17th Street, New York, New York 10011.

First printing: October 1994

Printed in the United States of America

HarperPaperbacks and colophon are trademarks of HarperCollins*Publishers*

10 9 8 7 6 5 4 3 2

1

ON A COLD JANUARY MORNING, SAMANTHA MCLEAN hoisted a pitchfork of soiled bedding into a wheelbarrow, then turned to the beautiful chestnut mare occupying one of the stalls at Whitebrook Farm.

"Okay, Wonder, scoot over. I need to do the other side." The Thoroughbred mare, who had been a champion racehorse before her retirement, obediently stepped to the other side of the roomy box stall. "That's a girl," Samantha said, patting Wonder's flank affectionately. Tossing her long red ponytail over her shoulder, Samantha got back to work with her pitchfork.

"Sammy?" a voice called from down the aisle. "Are you in here?"

Samantha poked her head out of the stall and saw Ashleigh Griffen approaching. "I'm over here, Ash, with Wonder."

"Hi," Ashleigh said with a smile as she hurried to the stall.

"What's up?" Samantha asked, noticing the excited sparkle in Ashleigh's hazel eyes.

Wonder, seeing her beloved owner, had stepped to the stall opening and was nudging Ashleigh eagerly with her nose. The two of them had shared a very special bond ever since Ashleigh's loving care had saved Wonder from sure death when she was a foal. Since then they had met challenge after challenge together during Wonder's career as a racer, and now as a broodmare. Just two months before Wonder had tragically lost her latest foal in a stillborn birth, and Ashleigh had been there for her.

"Hello, girl," Ashleigh crooned, gently rubbing the mare's velvety nose. Wonder responded with a loving whoof into Ashleigh's hand. "Yes, I'm glad to see you looking so good. I know you'd rather be out in the pasture, but it's icy out there today." Like Samantha, Ashleigh had pulled her dark brown hair back in a ponytail for practicality.

"Mike just called," Ashleigh said eagerly to Samantha. Six months before, Ashleigh had married her long-time boyfriend, Mike Reese, co-owner of Whitebrook, and the two of them seemed blissfully happy. "He's on his way back from that bankruptcy sale in New Jersey and will need us to help him unload the van."

"So he bought some horses," Samantha said with a touch of surprise. Neither she nor Ashleigh had expected Mike would find much at the sale. The owner of the New Jersey stable was a small-time, third-rate trainer who was selling everything to pay off bad gambling debts.

"Four of them," Ashleigh replied. "And he said he has a big surprise."

"Really?" Samantha's green eyes brightened with curiosity.

"Except he sounded funny—like he wasn't sure I'd like it." For an instant a frown marred Ashleigh's pretty face. At twenty-two, Ashleigh had recently gotten her full jockey's license. Her slim build made her ideally suited to the profession. She was also a licensed trainer, and therefore, for professional reasons, had kept her maiden name after her marriage to Mike.

"Well, you'll find out what it is soon," Samantha said cheerfully. She was looking forward to seeing the new stock Mike had purchased. "I'm just about finished," she added, forking the last of the soiled bedding into a wheelbarrow. Ashleigh gave Wonder a final pat and latched the stall door behind Samantha.

"I can't believe Mike would bring you a surprise you didn't like," Samantha told her as they set off down the aisle past the stalls of a half-dozen sleek Thoroughbred mares.

One tall black mare whickered to them as they passed her stall. Fleet Goddess had been another of Ashleigh's champion racers, but she was now heavy with a foal sired by Mike's prize stallion, Jazzman. Their first offspring, an adorable yearling filly aptly named Precocious, was stalled farther down the barn where the young horses were housed.

Ashleigh laughed. "Me neither. Gosh, he's only been gone three days, but I've missed him so much."

Seeing Ashleigh's smiling face, Samantha was

3

reminded that things hadn't been so rosy a few weeks before, when Wonder's firstborn, Wonder's Pride, had nearly died after suffering a twisted and ruptured intestine. Pride, who had just been named Horse of the Year, was Samantha's special horse. She'd groomed him since he was a yearling and exercise-ridden him in all his workouts. She'd joyfully shared in his victories and had been anticipating his five-year-old racing season. She would never forget the wrenching grief and agony she and Ashleigh had felt when the vet suggested they put Pride down.

And Pride's illness had only been the culmination of six months of tragedies. In July, Charlie Burke, the wise and trusted old trainer who had been Ashleigh's mentor, had died of a heart attack. Late in the fall Wonder's second-born filly, Townsend Princess, had been sidelined with a fractured leg. Then Wonder had lost her new foal.

But Pride had miraculously pulled through and was now on the road to recovery. Samantha was convinced that somehow he had known the vet's intentions to put him down and had fought back with an incredible display of will and courage. He was still recovering at the Lexington clinic, where he would remain until the vet was sure he was fully healed. But his racing career was over.

Samantha took a deep breath as she and Ashleigh stepped out into the cool, crystalline air of a Kentucky January day. Samantha loved Whitebrook. It was a beautiful farm, though not nearly as big as nearby Townsend Acres, the huge, famous breeding and racing farm where she and her father, not to mention Ashleigh and her family, had once lived. Clay Townsend, the owner of Townsend Acres, was co-owner with Ashleigh of Wonder and all her offspring, which frequently made for tension between the two farms. In fact, it was Clay Townsend's daughter-in-law, Lavinia, who had been responsible for Townsend Princess's injury. She had taken the two-year-old filly out on the training oval at Townsend Acres without permission. She didn't have the skill to handle Princess, and the filly bolted, fell, and fractured her leg. Lavinia had shown no guilt or remorse.

Samantha shook away any unpleasant thoughts as she followed Ashleigh out into the stable yard. The bare trees and rolling, snow-covered hills with white-fenced paddocks had a spare beauty that couldn't be matched. Across the stable yard was the white farmhouse Ashleigh and Mike shared with Mike's father, Gene Reese, who oversaw the breeding operation on the farm. To the left of the mares' barn was the large training barn, where the dozen or so horses in active training were kept. Beyond that was the mile training oval. Farther back was the smaller barn that housed the farm's four—soon to be five—stallions. When Pride returned to Whitebrook, he would be joining their ranks. The thought that he would never race again saddened Samantha. But at least her beloved horse was alive—that was all that really mattered.

"Here's Mike!" Ashleigh cried as the big Whitebrook horse van turned into the long, winding drive. When Mike pulled the van to a stop, Samantha and Ashleigh hurried over.

Mike swung down out of the cab, a wide smile lighting his face. His blond hair was pushed back casually over his forehead, and his blue eyes were shining as he greeted Ashleigh.

"Welcome home," Ashleigh said happily, running over to hug him and give him a welcoming kiss. "So what's this surprise?" she asked him eagerly.

For an instant, Mike looked a little hesitant. He walked to the side of the van while Vic Taleski, one of the young grooms Mike had hired after Charlie's death, unlatched and rolled aside the van doors. "Well, I bought some horses," he finally replied.

Ashleigh laughed. "I know. You told me. That can't be the surprise. You just want to keep me on pins and needles."

Mike gave her a sheepish smile. "Wait and see. It *will* be a surprise."

Ashleigh shrugged as Vic began leading the newly purchased horses out of the van.

By now, Samantha was very curious about Mike's surprise, too.

The first horse Vic led out was a big gray gelding. The first thing Samantha noticed was the terrible state of the horse's coat. He looked as if he hadn't been groomed for days, and he was much too thin. Generally before an auction, horses were spiffed up to look their absolute best. Ashleigh had noticed, too, and was frowning.

"This is Rocky Heights," Mike said. "He's a

6

lightly raced three-year-old, but his breeding is decent, and I think with some conditioning, he might have potential."

"Are all the horses in such bad shape?" Ashleigh asked with concern. "I hope you had a vet check him over!"

"You know I'd never buy a horse unless I had a vet check it," Mike said. "But I have to warn you, some of them are worse. Things must have been pretty bad at that stable in the last few weeks. None of the horses were getting proper care."

Len, the Reeses' longtime stable manager, came out of the barn to join them. The older black man had done a lot to help run things after Charlie's death.

"Welcome home!" he called cheerfully to Mike. "What have we here? Rocky, is it?" He approached the gray gelding. He too lifted his brows when he saw the gelding's condition, but he made no comment on it. "I think I can find a nice stall for you inside. Come on there, big guy."

Then Vic led two mares out of the van, a bay and a chestnut, both of which would also benefit from some tender loving care. "I bought these two as broodmares," Mike explained. "Neither of them did much on the track, but their breeding is good, too. They're basically sound, and a few weeks on a healthy diet will make a big difference in their appearance."

Samantha reminded herself that this was true, and she knew Mike wouldn't spend his hard-earned money on a sick animal with no potential. But she sure was surprised at Mike's purchases.

7

A moment later Vic led the last horse off the van, and both Samantha and Ashleigh gasped in horror. It was a roan filly, but the most pathetic specimen of a Thoroughbred that Samantha had ever seen. The filly was literally skin and bones. Her withers and hip-bones stuck out of her filthy coat like coat hangers under a blanket. Her shaggy coat of mixed dark red and white hairs had an unhealthy dullness. Her black mane and tail were a tangled mess. Her head hung listlessly as Vic led her forward, as if she hadn't the strength to hold it upright. She gazed at them from lifeless brown eyes that also had a hint of fear in them.

Ashleigh's mouth was open, and she seemed shocked into speechlessness.

"I know," Mike said quickly, seeing Ashleigh's expression. "She looks awful."

"She looks sick!" Ashleigh exclaimed. "I can't believe you bought her!"

"I had a very good reason," Mike said in a rush. "I know you'll find it hard to believe—but she's Wonder's half-sister."

"What!" Ashleigh and Samantha cried in one breath. "But how . . ." Ashleigh stuttered. "I mean . . . look at her . . . she couldn't be . . ."

"I know, I know," Mike said. "I wasn't even considering buying her until I saw her pedigree. I couldn't believe it myself."

Samantha had stepped closer to the bedraggled filly. She laid a gentle hand on the filly's shoulder and felt the muscles twitch nervously beneath her hand. Obviously the young horse didn't have much trust in

8

humans. It didn't seem possible that this sad example of neglect and ill-treatment could possibly be related to Wonder, who was the very definition of Thoroughbred breeding.

"Wonder and this filly were both sired by Townsend Pride," Mike continued. "Of course, Wonder is six years older. This filly turned three on January 1."

"How could a daughter of Townsend Pride end up in such a third-rate stable?" Samantha asked in amazement. Townsend Pride was one of the top stallions at Townsend Acres—in the country, for that matter. His stud fees were astronomical, and the foals he sired went to only the best stables. Clay Townsend was always extremely careful about Townsend Pride's stud book and the mares that were bred to him.

"It's a sad story," Mike said. "Her dam, Brite Morn, was sent down from a Maryland farm to be bred to Townsend Pride. The filly was foaled on the Maryland farm the next spring and was sent to auction as a yearling. She was purchased by a small Maryland stable, but before she went into serious training, the stable came on hard times, and she was sold again. From then on, it was all downhill." Mike shook his head. "From what I could learn, she was raced this past summer as a two-year-old on the small-track circuit. She didn't win any races, and she obviously wasn't treated well. The New Jersey trainer got her out of a claiming race for nearly nothing a few months ago. Right after that the trainer went bankrupt, and all his horses suffered."

"But she looks like she's been practically starved to death!" Ashleigh exclaimed.

"Like I said, her owner went bankrupt," Mike explained. "He obviously wasn't forking out any money for feed or stable help."

"It's a crime to treat a horse like that!" Ashleigh said angrily. She went over to the filly and looked her up and down. "What's her name?"

Mike smiled ruefully. "It's Shining. I know—she looks anything but shining now. But I'm hoping once we fatten her up and give her some decent care, her bloodlines will show through. Her dam never raced, but her great-grandsire was Bold Ruler. And if the mare hadn't had a decent pedigree, Townsend Acres never would have accepted her for breeding."

"You poor thing," Samantha said softly. She studied the filly more carefully. Despite Shining's pitiable appearance, Samantha thought she could see a hint of good breeding in the filly's finely shaped head, wide-set eyes, long, straight legs, and breadth of chest. If properly cared for, her roan coloring could be eye-catching, too. Beneath the dirt crusting her coat, Shining was an even-toned red roan. The white and rust-colored hairs on her back and sides shaded to black on her legs and muzzle. Her mane and tail were black, too, and someday could flow like silk.

Samantha gently rubbed her hand down Shining's neck. The filly shuddered again as if she were expecting pain, not pleasure. Samantha's mouth tightened angrily at the thought of the abuse the filly must have suffered.

"She's on the small side, too," Samantha said with a frown. Shining stood about fifteen hands—not very tall for a Thoroughbred mare.

"When's her actual birth date?" Samantha asked Mike. Although all Thoroughbreds' official birthday was January 1, their actual birth date could be months later, in the spring.

"She was foaled in May—a late foal," Mike answered.

"So she could still grow a little," Samantha said.

"I wouldn't be surprised if her growth was stunted because of poor diet," Ashleigh speculated unhappily.

Finally, as Samantha continued to rub the filly's neck, Shining turned her head to look at Samantha with soft brown eyes. Samantha sensed there was entreaty in that look, as if the filly were begging for some compassion and affection. Samantha's heart went out to her completely. In that instant she determined to do everything in her power to bring Shining back to health.

Glancing up, Samantha met Ashleigh's gaze. She saw the same distress and desire to help in Ashleigh's eyes. "It's going to be okay, girl," she whispered to Shining. "We're going to take good care of you here. You won't have to worry anymore."

"A warm bath would be a good start," Ashleigh said.

Samantha nodded, then quietly groaned. "If things weren't bad enough, you poor thing, you've got lice."

"I know," Mike said unhappily. "When the vet checked her over, he also said she'd need worming. That's part of the reason she's skin and bones. I'll call our own vet and have him come take a look at her.

Meanwhile we'll keep her in the isolation stall—I don't want the other horses infected. If she hadn't been Wonder's half-sister, I would have passed on her. But the alternative was probably a meat-packing plant."

Samantha felt sick at the thought.

"You did the right thing in bringing her home, Mike," Ashleigh said firmly. "You couldn't have left her to a fate like that. She'll probably never race again, but we can sure try to get her fit and healthy. She deserves a good home."

Mike smiled and gave Ashleigh's shoulders a loving squeeze. "I thought you'd feel that way, Ash. It's going to be a long struggle, though, considering the condition she's in."

"We can do it," Samantha said with conviction. "I'd like to take responsibility for her." As she said the words, she knew how much she meant them. A few weeks earlier, when Pride had been close to death, she'd wondered if she would ever have the strength to care for a sick horse again. But now, looking at the ill-treated filly, she was suddenly filled with a new determination. There would be hard work and possible disappointment ahead, but she knew she had to at least try to help Shining.

"Are you sure you want to?" Ashleigh asked with concern. "I know you've done amazing things with other horses, but she's going to need a lot of time and attention. After all she's been through—and we can only guess the extent of it—your hard work might not pay off."

Samantha didn't hesitate. "I want to do it. And with Pride at the clinic, I have the time."

Shining turned her head and gave Samantha another sad look, and Samantha was more sure than ever.

After a brief glance at Mike, Ashleigh nodded, a look of relief crossing her face. She smiled. "Okay, Sammy. In a way, I'm glad you want to. Mike and I will be leaving next week for the Caribbean—we're finally going to have our honeymoon! I won't have the time to devote to Shining. I just want you to realize that it's not going to be easy. You have to be prepared for the possibility that she may never snap back. We may be too late."

"But we may not," Samantha replied. "And I couldn't bear not to try."

ASHLEIGH HELPED SAMANTHA SETTLE SHINING IN THE quarantine stall at the rear of the mares' barn. They tried to make the filly as comfortable as possible, bringing her fresh water and hay. Shining drank deeply from the water bucket but ignored the hay. Ashleigh and Samantha exchanged a worried look.

"She's not used to her new surroundings," Ashleigh said. "She'll start eating once she settles in."

Silently Samantha hoped that was true.

A few minutes later Mike's vet, Dr. Mendez, arrived to give Shining a thorough examination. Samantha held Shining's head as the vet examined her. Mike and Ashleigh waited outside the stall. When Dr. Mendez had finished, he turned to Mike and shook his head. "I'll give you worming medication for her, but I hope you realized what you were getting into when you bought this filly. You've got a long road ahead bringing her back to health. She's been badly neglected."

Mike nodded. "We know, but she's got the best caretaker she can get in Sammy." He looked over at Samantha and smiled.

Dr. Mendez looked in Samantha's direction, too. "Well, I certainly remember one of the miracles you pulled off." He smiled. "I never thought Wonder's Pride would make it, but he's getting better every day. Let's hope you can work another miracle with this horse."

"I'm going to try," Samantha said firmly.

"Good. With her bloodlines, it would be a shame to lose her."

Lose her? Samantha thought. She hadn't even considered the possibility. And she wasn't going to now, either!

For the rest of the afternoon, Samantha worked on Shining. She got some antilice spray from the supply room, then put Shining in crossties and sprayed her thoroughly. After putting on rubber gloves, she rubbed the de-licer into Shining's coat, then sprayed her again. She had no intention of letting a single parasite survive.

Next she lathered the filly up with warm soapy water, working the lather into Shining's roan coat with her fingertips. With warm water from the hose she rinsed Shining off carefully, making sure that no soapy residue remained. The filly stood quietly, barely reacting as the warm water sluiced over her.

Samantha then took a sweat strap to Shining's coat, removing as much moisture as possible. She finished the drying process by rubbing her down with

16

clean, absorbent cotton towels. Then she began the laborious task of trying to groom the worst of the dead hair and dead lice from the filly's coat. Starting with Shining's neck, she worked a currycomb in a circular motion over the shaggy coat, stopping frequently to clean the comb of dead hair.

Samantha knew it would take more than one grooming to make Shining's coat even moderately presentable, but today would be a start. And Shining seemed to enjoy the massaging pressure of the brush stimulating her circulation. It had obviously been a long time since anyone had given her such a thorough grooming—or any attention at all. Samantha's mouth tightened angrily. Then she heard the filly's barely audible grunt of pleasure, and smiled.

After she'd curried Shining, Samantha went over the filly's coat again with a moderately soft brush, smoothing the hairs into place. With the worst of the grime removed, Samantha could begin to see that the horse's dark red coloring, sprinkled with white, would be beautiful. The soft black of her legs and nose added a pleasing contrast. Her black mane and tail, though, were still a tangled mess.

Some of the tangles were so bad that Samantha was forced to cut them out with scissors. She tried to even out the raggedy edges of what remained, but the result definitely wasn't a work of beauty. She consoled herself that Shining's mane and tail would grow out again eventually, and at least now they were tangle free.

Len came in to check Samantha's progress.

17

"Well, the little lady does look better," he said.

Samantha smiled. "You don't have to say it, Len. She still has a long way to go."

"But you're making a start. It'll take patience and time. How are her feet?" he asked.

Samantha had lifted one of Shining's forelegs and was using a hoofpick to remove embedded dirt from the frog of the hoof. "A mess. Her hooves need trimming badly before they crack, and she'll need to be reshod."

"I'll call Tamara Wilson in the morning," Len promised, speaking of Whitebrook's regular farrier. "She'll fix her up."

Samantha finished cleaning Shining's hind hooves, then stood. "I'm going to blanket her and let her rest," she said as she unclipped the crossties from Shining's halter and led her into the stall. Samantha had already collected a clean, padded horse blanket from the tack room, and now she belted it around the filly. The de-licer and bath had removed some of the natural protective oils from Shining's coat, and Samantha didn't want the filly to get chilled.

Len stepped into the stall and walked over to Shining. He laid a gentle, weathered hand on her neck. The filly trembled in fear, although Len's touch was soothing and kind. "Just take it easy, sweetheart," he murmured reassuringly. "No one's going to hurt you. From here on out, all you're going to get is love."

Shining anxiously flicked her ears and eyed Len. She obviously wasn't ready to trust anyone yet.

"The other problem is she's not eating," Samantha said to Len. "She wouldn't even go near her hay net before. You'd think she'd be starving. Ashleigh said we should give her time to settle in. What do you think?"

"You might need to tempt her, but you can't give her anything too rich," Len said, rubbing his chin thoughtfully. "She's not used to it and might colic. How about if I cook up a nice hot bran mash for her? If she takes to that, we can mix some corn into her regular feed. I'll start her on vitamins—that concentrated supplement we have in the back."

Samantha nodded. "Horse chow."

"As far as her coat goes," Len added, "I'll boil up some linseed and make a paste you can mix in with her feed morning and night. In a month, her coat may even be shining again and we'll have her living up to her name. I'll start her on the worming medication tonight. Other than that, just keep her hay net and water bucket full. We'll hope for the best."

"Thanks, Len," Samantha said gratefully.

"If you need any help or advice," Len added, "just let me know. I'd like to see this pretty little lady come back into her own, too."

That night when Samantha entered the small cottage she shared with her father, Ian McLean, she was tired, sweaty, and filthy. Her father and Beth Raines were both in the kitchen, preparing the meal.

"Hi, Dad. Hi, Beth," Samantha said. "Something

19

sure smells good. Let me just take a quick shower and I'll be down to set the table."

"Okay, honey," her father said, and Beth smiled her agreement.

As Samantha trudged upstairs, she thought about how her relationship with Beth had changed over the last six months. Samantha's mother had died almost five years earlier, and Beth was the first woman Mr. McLean had dated since becoming a widower. At first Samantha had been angry and resentful, especially since Beth knew nothing about horses—she was an aerobics instructor in Lexington. For a while, Samantha's relationship with her father had suffered. But slowly she was starting to appreciate Beth, and to like her, and to be glad of the happiness Beth had brought her father.

At dinner Mr. McLean said, "I stopped in to look at Mike's new horses. I hear you've taken on that beat-up little filly."

Samantha helped herself to some green beans and nodded. "I just know there's more to her than meets the eye, Dad. After all, she's Wonder's half-sister. That must mean something."

Beth smiled at her across the table. "I know what you mean, Sammy. I felt the same way the first time I saw my class of physically challenged kids. One look at their hopeful faces, and I could see past the wheelchairs and the leg braces—right into the athletes they wanted to become."

In addition to the regular aerobics classes that Beth taught at the studio she co-owned with Janet Roarsh,

she also taught several groups of children with physi-
cal disabilities. With her help Samantha and her boyfriend, Tor Nelson, had started a pony-riding class for
six of the children at Tor's riding stable.

Samantha nodded. "Right. So you do understand."

Mr. McLean frowned. "Sammy, I don't want to discourage you, but that horse is in bad shape. I don't
want you to get your hopes up too high in case nothing comes of all your time and trouble."

Samantha shook her head confidently. "Don't
worry, Dad."

"So when do you leave for Florida?" Beth asked
Ian McLean.

"Next week. Normally Mike would take his string
of racers down to the Gulfstream track, but he and
Ashleigh will be on their honeymoon. You should
think about trying to come down to meet me one
weekend." His eyes twinkled at Beth, and Samantha
ducked her head to hide her private smile.

"Maybe I will. After all, you'll be gone for six long
weeks, right? And I haven't been to Florida in a long
time. I'm ready for a little sunshine and warmth."

"It's a deal, then."

After taking another sip of milk, Samantha
glanced at her watch. "Oh, gosh—can I be excused?
Tor will be here any second, and my hair is still wet!"

Her father laughed and waved her off.

Samantha brought Tor out to the barn to see
Shining before they left for the movies in Lexington.
She saw his face fall when he got a good look at the

filly, even though he tried his best to hide it, and she felt a stab of disappointment.

"I know she looks pretty bad," Samantha said quickly, "but she's Wonder's half-sister. With love and decent care, I know she'll bounce back."

At the moment Shining was standing at the very rear of her stall, putting as much distance between herself and them as possible. She eyed Tor—a new stranger—with fear, and that skittish fear did nothing to improve her appearance.

"I guess I wasn't expecting her to be in quite such bad shape," Tor admitted. He softened his statement by putting his arm around Samantha's shoulders. "I can understand why Mike brought her home, though. He wouldn't have left a half-sister of Wonder's to a miserable fate, but after so much neglect, I don't know how she can ever come back one hundred percent. You're taking on a lot here, Sammy."

Samantha's feeling of disappointment grew. Tor knew horses inside out and backwards. With his father, he co-owned a riding stable in Lexington and competed with his horse, Top Hat, on the show-jumping circuit at the top levels. Samantha had been so sure that he would see beyond Shining's present pathetic state to the animal she could become with proper care.

Tor glanced down and saw her expression, then smiled. "That's not to say I don't think you can do it," he said softly. "When you set your mind to something, you almost always succeed."

Samantha returned his smile. "All right. That's better."

"Good. I didn't mean to discourage you. Let's go meet Yvonne and Gregg," he said, giving her shoulders a squeeze. "They'll be waiting for us outside the theater."

When the four friends left the theater two hours later, they walked to a nearby coffee bar and found a table.

"Not the greatest movie, was it?" Yvonne asked, pushing her straight black hair behind her ear and taking a sip of the cappuccino the waitress placed in front of her.

"I sure was disappointed," Gregg agreed. His auburn curls contrasted sharply with Yvonne's dark hair. "Talk about slow. It seemed like we were in the theater for hours. Oh well, win some, lose some. At least we'll know not to rent the video."

"Sammy," Tor said with a twinkle in his blue eyes. "You haven't told Yvonne your big news."

Samantha hadn't said anything about Shining yet, feeling unwilling to hear discouraging comments from Yvonne and Gregg, although Yvonne was as big a softie as she was when it came to needy animals. Yvonne and Gregg were both riders and took lessons from Tor. Yvonne was doing spectacularly well, and Tor was encouraging her to compete in the National Horse Show at the beginning of March.

Yvonne's almond-shaped black eyes widened slightly. "What big news? Tell, tell!"

Samantha took a sip from her cup. "Mike bought some new horses today." She paused. "One of them is a roan filly—a half-sister to Wonder."

"What?" Yvonne gasped, leaning across the table. "You're kidding! Where did he find her?"

Quickly Samantha told them the story of how Mike had found Shining.

"I can't wait to see her," Yvonne said excitedly.

Samantha grimaced. "Be warned: she needs some TLC." She described the poor state of the filly's health.

"But if anyone can bring her up to scratch, Sammy can," Tor said loyally, smiling over at Samantha.

"Let me know if I can help," Yvonne offered instantly.

"I think you're going to be pretty busy training for the National Horse Show," Samantha reminded her.

"Well, yeah, but I'm sure I'll have *some* time available," Yvonne said.

"I can't believe you qualify to enter the National Horse Show. It's so exciting," Gregg told her, squeezing her hand on the table.

Yvonne grinned at him. "Good. Then you won't mind coming to the stable to keep me company when Cisco and I practice tomorrow afternoon. Beth's kids are coming in the morning, too, aren't they?" she asked Tor.

For the last couple of months, all four of them had been working with the six physically challenged children Beth had introduced them to, teaching them to ride at Tor's stable. Beth and her partner brought the children to the stable every other week, and so far the lessons had been a huge success, giving the children a feeling of mobility they didn't have in their wheelchairs or on crutches.

"I've come up with a great name for the class," Tor said with a grin. "I think we should call them the Pony Commandos. What do you guys think?"

"The kids will love it!" Yvonne cried, grinning too. "It will make them feel really important. Maybe we could have T-shirts made up."

"Not a bad idea," Tor agreed. "Let me talk it over with Beth and Janet." He glanced at his watch. "Uh-oh, Sammy. Time to bring you home. I didn't realize it was so late. And we'll both have a busy morning."

"I guess we'd better make a move, too," Gregg said. They all put on their coats and went outside into the cold night air. "See you tomorrow," Yvonne called as they waved their good-byes. "And after I practice with Cisco, I want to come over and see the new filly," she added to Samantha.

"Anytime," Samantha told her.

When they reached Whitebrook, Tor walked Samantha to the cottage door and gave her a warm good-night kiss. "See you tomorrow," he said. Then he touched his finger affectionately to the end of her nose.

Samantha smiled up at him. "Not that I'm in any hurry to go in—only *you* could make hanging around in freezing weather appealing. But you're right—" She smothered a yawn. "Time to get some sleep." They exchanged a last kiss, and Tor turned and headed down the walk. With a smile, Samantha slipped into the darkened, silent house. She heard Tor's truck driving off into the night.

In her own room, she sleepily started to get undressed, then had a sudden impulse to check on

25

Shining one last time. Quickly she shoved her feet into her stable boots and threw on her jacket again.

Creeping downstairs silently was easy, and she let herself out the back door without a sound. The dried, dead grass of the stable yard was stiff with frost as she crunched her way to the mares' barn. Her breath made little white puffs in the chilly night air, and the breeze brushed her cheeks.

The door to the mares' barn opened easily, and Samantha padded down the main aisle of the stable, breathing in the air that smelled sweetly of fresh hay, leather, and the warm, clean scent of contented horses. Mike's mares were all dozing peacefully, their breaths puffing softly in the dim light.

When Samantha reached Shining's stall, she peered over the wall cautiously, not wanting to disturb the young horse. But Shining was awake in an instant, her brown eyes wide as she nervously looked to see who was there.

"It's okay, girl," Samantha said softly. She lifted the latch to the stall door and let herself inside. Shining didn't skitter nervously, but she didn't come forward, either. Samantha stepped through the straw on the floor and came to lay a gentle hand on Shining's clean neck. The filly whoofed out a breath and kept a watchful eye on Samantha's movements.

"There, there," Samantha soothed, gently stroking the filly's neck. She scratched between Shining's ears, which were drooping to each side, and softly rubbed her delicate nose. Samantha noticed happily that the bran mash Len had made for the filly was nearly gone. But looking into Shining's mistrustful dark eyes, Samantha felt a twinge of uncertainty. Could Shining be made to trust again? What had Samantha taken on? She knew that without Shining's trust and cooperation, nothing could ever come of the filly. No matter how hard Samantha worked, it might all come to nothing, as her father had warned her—the horse might never race again, might never show the slightest spark of the talent or drive that had made her half-sister famous.

Samantha shook her head firmly. She wasn't going to think like that. She gently kissed Shining's smooth neck. "I know we can do it, girl," she whispered. "You and me—we'll show everybody! You'll just *have* to learn to trust me. In the meantime, eat up and rest up. You deserve it."

3

"WHEW! IT'S CHILLY OUT THERE!" SAMANTHA EXCLAIMED as she hurried into the big indoor ring at Tor's stable on Sunday morning.

Tor looked up from where he was tightening the saddle girth on a short, fat pony. When he saw Samantha, he grinned. "Maybe you need some special Tor Nelson warm-up treatment," he said, giving her a mock-wicked look.

Samantha rolled her eyes, picked up a saddle, and walked over to another pony.

Tor laughed, showing his even white teeth. He finished tightening the saddle girth and patted the pony on the rump. "Okay, Butterball." He led the pony over to the side of the ring, where two other saddled ponies were waiting.

Samantha finished tacking up Zorro, an ambitiously named small pony with gentle eyes and a fuzzy black coat. Then she started on Milk Dud.

The large indoor ring was meticulously tidied as usual. The dirt had been raked smooth, and all the jumping equipment was dismantled and piled neatly at one end. Before the jumping classes started later that afternoon, Tor and his father would reconstruct the jumps around the ring.

It was quiet now, the only sounds being the soft stamping of small pony feet against the deep dirt and the gentle whooshing of their breaths, but Samantha knew that later on, when the people who boarded horses with Tor came to exercise them, the ring would be full of noise and activity.

"Ah! Here come the Pony Commandos," Tor called cheerfully.

Beth Raines and her partner, Janet Roarsh, came in, each wheeling a small child in an undersize wheelchair. Two other kids were walking slowly and clumsily with leg braces and crutches, and parents were helping in the last two children. There were three boys, Timmy Alonso, Robert Simon, and Aaron Fineberg, and three girls, Mandy Jarvis, Charmaine Green, and Jane McKendrick. All the kids were about seven years old.

"Hi, Mandy," Samantha said with a big smile, going over to one of her favorite students. Mandy was a spunky six-year-old who had been in a bad car accident the year before. Her legs had been severely damaged, and though she was making gradual progress and hoped to walk normally someday, she was still hampered by her heavy leg braces.

"Hi, Samantha!" Mandy waved excitedly, her dark

eyes shining. Her father was guiding her to the outside of the ring.

Samantha led over Butterball, and Mr. Jarvis helped Mandy get settled in the saddle. Her small, smooth brown hands gripped the reins as Samantha had shown her.

Smiling at Mr. Jarvis, Samantha said, "Mandy is a natural horsewoman."

Mandy's face split into a huge, delighted smile.

Soon Yvonne and Gregg showed up, and there was a flurry of activity as the six kids all got settled comfortably in their saddles. Then the six adults, Beth, Janet, Tor, Samantha, Gregg, and Yvonne, each led a pony and rider around the ring. First they went at a slow walk, then a brisker walk, then Tor cried, "Are you ready to trot?"

"Yes!" the children responded.

Samantha led Butterball around the ring in a nicely paced jog, turning around now and then to make sure Mandy had a good seat and was holding on. Her thin legs were almost useless at gripping Butterball's round sides, but still, she sat deeply in the saddle, her back straight, her eyes forward. Her hands gripped some of Butterball's mane for stability.

They continued to lead the ponies around the big ring and progressed to trotting in figure eights. Then Tor split the class into two groups so the children could practice walking their ponies around the ring without being led.

When the class finally came to an end, over the kids' disappointed protests, Samantha said, "I'm really proud of you, Mandy. You're a terrific rider. Even some kids who don't wear leg braces don't ride as well as you."

The small girl beamed, then said in a serious voice, "I love horses—I love everything about them. When I get better, I'll start riding big horses, not ponies. And then I'll ride racehorses. And then—" She broke off as Samantha laughed at her enthusiasm.

"I bet you will!" Samantha declared, leaning over to give her a hug. "It takes nerve, courage, and determination, and you have all those."

Mandy kissed Butterball good-bye, and Samantha heard her talking excitedly to her father about her lesson. She watched Mandy leave with a pang in her heart. It was true that Mandy had grit and determination—but Samantha knew it took more than that to ride racehorses. And she didn't know if Mandy's legs would ever be strong enough.

Samantha steered her father's car down the long gravel drive to Whitebrook. She had picked up a few things at the grocery store after school, since this was her father's last night at home before leaving for Florida. Samantha had planned a special meal. It would be just the two of them, like old times, because Beth was teaching an evening aerobics class. Selfishly, Samantha felt glad. As much as she now enjoyed Beth's company, it was nice to have her father to herself once in a while.

But she groaned as she braked the car to a stop in front of the cottage. Across the stable yard, Lavinia and Brad Townsend were climbing out of Brad's Ferrari. As usual they made a spectacularly attractive couple, Brad's dark good looks contrasting with Lavinia's blond ones. *If only beauty were more than skin deep,* Samantha thought.

These two had caused Ashleigh and Samantha nothing but trouble, especially in the last year when, in a desperate attempt to prevent Pride from beating their own horse, Lord Ainsley, they had tried one dirty trick after another to get Pride out of the picture.

Samantha left the groceries in the car and followed Lavinia and Brad toward the mares' barn. Ashleigh and Mike were doing some last-minute shopping before they left for the Caribbean. Mr. Reese had gone to pick up feed, and her father had a dentist appointment. She and Len were the only ones there to keep an eye on the young Townsends.

She was sure they'd come to check on Wonder's yearling, Mr. Wonderful, the beautifully conformed colt who was showing all the spunk his brother, Wonder's Pride, had shown at that age.

Neither Brad nor Lavinia actually owned any interest in Wonder and her offspring—Brad's father did—but that didn't stop them from coming over to Whitebrook as if they owned the place and butting in with their unwanted opinions.

As she entered the barn, Samantha heard Lavinia's haughty voice drifting over from the direction of Wonder's stall. "She definitely should be bred to another stallion this year," Lavinia was telling Brad.

"She's lost two foals sired by Baldasar. It's time for new blood."

As if you know anything about breeding horses, Lavinia, Samantha thought angrily. Although Lavinia was from a very wealthy family who had always kept horses for pleasure riding, breeding and training Thoroughbred racehorses was a completely different proposition. It irked Samantha no end that Lavinia continually tried to force her unknowledgeable decisions on Ashleigh. And Samantha was still furious that Lavinia was responsible for possibly ruining all racing prospects for Townsend Princess.

"I've talked to my father," Brad said. "He's considering it."

"Good," Lavinia replied. "He really has to do something."

As Samantha slowly came down the aisle, she saw Brad look around with interest at some of the other stalls. Neither of them had noticed her yet, so they probably felt free to do a little spying.

"I see some mares I don't recognize," Brad said.

"I heard a rumor that Mike had gone up to a sale at some decrepit stable in New Jersey," Lavinia replied. "I can't imagine he could have found anything decent—definitely nothing like the two mares we just bought. Which of these are new?"

Brad motioned. "That bay and that chestnut."

Lavinia made a sour face. "They're nothing special."

Len had quietly come down the aisle from the rear of the barn. He didn't like Brad and Lavinia any more than Samantha did. "Something I can help you

34

with?" Len asked. Lavinia and Brad turned to him. Samantha took the opportunity to walk past them to Shining's stall.

"I don't think so," Lavinia said dismissively. She turned away as if she owned Whitebrook and continued down the aisle. Samantha had quietly let herself into Shining's stall. The last thing she needed was to have Lavinia and Brad upsetting the filly. Shining was already cowering at the back of her stall in response to the strange voices.

Samantha tried to soothe her. "Don't pay any attention to them," she whispered. "I won't let them near you."

Samantha gritted her teeth when she heard the brittle tapping of Lavinia's heels approaching. She had been working so hard to give Shining a sense of security. She wasn't about to let Lavinia ruin that now.

But when she glanced up, Lavinia was looking over the stall door. "Oh, my God, what do you call that?" Lavinia asked, staring at Shining. Shining had started to tremble. Samantha felt like strangling Lavinia. "Don't tell me this is one of the new horses?" Lavinia added with a derisive chuckle.

Samantha gave her a level, unflinching look. "Okay, I won't tell you."

Lavinia sputtered with laughter. "You can't be serious! That horse looks like she's one step away from the glue factory. Brad, come here, you have to see this. Mike and Ashleigh must be absolutely desperate!"

"And what would you know, Lavinia?" Samantha

asked in cold anger. "You can barely tell the front of a horse from the back."

Lavinia's blue eyes narrowed. "And you're nothing but a lousy groom!"

Len and Brad had both walked up. "Mike's mares really aren't any of your business," Len said, giving Lavinia a hard look. "You're upsetting the filly."

Lavinia gave a tinkling laugh. "She already looks like she's at death's door."

"Maybe this little lady needs some TLC," Len responded, "but we think she's worth it."

"Oh?" Lavinia said archly. "And what makes her worth it?"

Samantha cast Len a pleading look. She didn't want him to reveal Shining's background to Brad or Lavinia. As pathetic as the filly looked now, Samantha knew Brad would take an instant interest in her if he knew she had been sired by Townsend Pride.

Len seemed to understand her look. "We have our reasons," he said vaguely.

Brad was looking in at Shining with a thoughtful, appraising frown, for once disagreeing with his wife. "I wouldn't underestimate Mike," he said almost under his breath. "He must have had some reason for buying her."

"Dog food?" Lavinia asked cheerfully.

Brad looked at his watch. "We'd better get going. Dad's plane will be in soon."

"We've seen enough here anyway." Lavinia turned, and ignoring Samantha and Len, sauntered off beside her husband.

When they were gone, Samantha and Len exchanged a relieved glance. "Whew!" Len said. "I'm glad to see the back of them."

"You handled it well," Samantha told him.

Len's face cracked in a pleased smile. "Yeah, well, we didn't want them disturbing this girl, now, did we?"

Samantha grinned back. "Keep them away from me, too, while you're at it."

With a laugh, Len headed back up the aisle toward the barn office. Samantha stayed with Shining a while longer, calming her down before returning to the car to unload the groceries.

At four thirty the next morning Samantha was up, dressed, and sleepily eating a bowl of instant oatmeal at the kitchen table. Although she got up early every day in order to take care of the horses and to exercise ride the ones Mike had in training, she was up extra early today to say good-bye to her father.

She could hear him out in the stable yard, loading up the big six-horse Whitebrook van. This winter Mike had a string of only four horses that he was sending to Florida for the Gulfstream races. Blues King, the horse who had won the Breeders' Cup Sprint last spring, was the only one that they were really counting on to do well. The others were going for the experience. The kitchen door opened and Ian McLean strode in, rubbing his hands together briskly and blowing on them. "It's chilly out there," he greeted his daughter. "You bundle up when you go ride."

"Okay, Dad," Samantha agreed.

"Listen, Sammy," her father said, pulling out a kitchen chair and sitting down. "I've left you a list of the phone numbers for my hotel and the stables at the racetrack, in case you need me. At any rate, I'll probably be calling almost every night to say hello." He gave her a wistful smile. "We haven't really been separated before, have we?"

Samantha shook her head.

"You won't be scared, staying in this house by yourself, huh?" Her father looked worried. "You know Gene Reese will still be here, over at the farmhouse."

"I'll be okay." Samantha tried to sound confident. "After all, I am seventeen."

"It's just that Ash and Mike will be leaving soon, too." Mr. McLean rubbed his face against his hand, as though starting to worry about Samantha already.

"Dad, I'll be fine," Samantha insisted.

"Well, you go stay with Yvonne if you get too lonesome, all right? I've already checked with her folks, and it's okay with them."

"Okay."

"Listen, Sammy," her father continued. To Samantha's amazement, a slow blush started creeping up his face. "You're going to be here on your own for a few weeks. You're a big girl, and I trust you. I always have."

What is he talking about? Samantha wondered. *He knows Len can take care of the stables.*

"You and Tor have been seeing each other for a long time now, and I know he's a nice guy—" Mr.

McLean stopped, seeming unsure of how to continue.

Suddenly Samantha got the point of this talk, and her eyes almost bugged out of her head.

"I mean, I know you care about each other—" Mr. McLean plowed on determinedly, clearly embarrassed but feeling his paternal duty strongly.

"Dad!" Samantha shrieked. "What are you talking about? Yes, Tor and I are dating, but we're not—I mean, we would never—I mean, there's no way—" She was so mortified, she could hardly speak. "Just because you're out of town doesn't mean—"

She knew her face was flushing. She knew where her father was coming from, but it was so embarrassing to hear him discuss her and Tor's relationship. She covered her face with her hands.

"Well, all right, then," Mr. McLean said cheerfully, standing up and patting her shoulder. "I'm glad we had this little talk. I feel much better, don't you?"

"Mumph," Samantha grunted, her face still hidden.

"Gosh, I better get going," he said brightly, heading for the door. "Want to hit the road early. Will you come see me off?"

Samantha got to her feet and grabbed her jacket. Her face was still burning, but she was also feeling a little amused. Her dad was so funny sometimes. She plunged out into the frigid morning air to say goodbye to him and to Vic, who was going with him.

JUST TWO DAYS LATER SAMANTHA WAS SAYING ANOTHER good-bye, this time to Ashleigh and Mike.

"Did you pack your bathing suit?" she asked Ashleigh.

Laughing, Ashleigh nodded. "It'll be strange to leave this winter weather and go someplace hot and sunny for three weeks."

"Well, you two deserve a break," Samantha declared. "You've been going nonstop since your wedding." Privately she thought about all the trials Ashleigh and Mike had faced in the last six months.

"It's a new year," Ashleigh said, smiling as she watched Mike load their luggage into their car. Len was going to drive them to the airport. "And that means new beginnings. Listen, Sammy, I wanted to talk to you before we go."

Samantha looked over. "Are you worried about how we're going to manage while you're gone?"

41

Frowning, Ashleigh shook her head. "Of course not. You're responsibility personified. No, it's about Shining," Ashleigh continued. Mike came up and put his arm around Ashleigh, and she turned to smile at him.

"Mike and I have been talking about Shining," Ashleigh said. "And about how much you've done for us over the years. First with Fleet Goddess, then with Pride—and now you've taken on the care of Shining, almost single-handedly. We've had some good years lately, and a large part of our success has been due to your hard work, commitment, and loyalty."

Blushing, Samantha looked down at the ground. She had only done it because she cared.

"Shining may not ever go back to racing," Ashleigh said. "But if anyone can work miracles with her, it will be you. Sammy, we'd like you to have her." Ashleigh stepped close and put a hand on each of Samantha's shoulders. "We're signing over Shining's papers to you. If nothing else, she'll make a good pleasure horse, and maybe a broodmare someday. She's yours now, with our love and thanks."

For a moment Samantha felt her head whirl dizzily as she stared at Ashleigh. *I must have misheard her. It almost sounded like . . .*

"Don't you want her?" Ashleigh teased, smiling.

"You—you don't mean . . . you mean that Shining is mine?" Samantha gasped. "She's my horse?"

Now Mike laughed. "Every inch of her. You deserve it, Sammy. And she deserves you."

"I . . . I . . ." Samantha was literally speechless. Her

mind was still spinning, thinking of all the possibilities at once. Her own horse, her very own . . .

"And don't you even think of offering to pay for her feed and board," Mike said sternly, shaking his finger at Samantha. "It's on us, and so are the vet bills. You've put in more than your share of unpaid labor."

"Oh, my God," Samantha gasped, the reality starting to sink in. For nearly five years she had loved Pride as if he were her own, and she'd cared for and loved Fleet Goddess and Wonder as if they were her own, too. But in her heart she'd always known they weren't hers. As much as she loved them, other people would make the decisions about their futures—not her. But now she did have a horse—a Thoroughbred of her own! "Oh, thank you! Thank you both!" she cried, throwing her arms around Ashleigh and giving her a fierce and grateful hug. Then she turned and hugged Mike as well. When she pulled away, happy tears welled up in her eyes. "I can't believe it. My own horse. I just can't believe it," she kept repeating.

"Believe it," Ashleigh said firmly. Then she glanced at her watch. "Oh, Mike, we have to go. Our plane is leaving in two hours, and we have to get to the airport!"

After more hugs and kisses, Samantha and Mr. Reese stood in the driveway and waved at the car until it turned onto the highway. For a few long moments Samantha just stood there, trying to absorb the fact that Shining was now hers. She was realizing, too, that for the first time she was going to be living

43

on her own in the cottage. Although two day grooms would come by in the morning to help muck the stalls, the only ones left on the farm were Mr. Reese, Len, and herself. It was a very strange feeling.

"I sure hope they have a good time," Mr. Reese said. "They're a great couple, aren't they?"

"The best."

"Well," Mr. Reese said cheerfully, "I guess I have some horses to look after. See you later, Sammy. If you get lonesome around dinnertime, just come over to the farmhouse. I've invited Len to join me, and we'd love the company."

"Thanks, Mr. Reese. My dad left me enough frozen food to feed an army for a month, but maybe I'll take you up on your offer. Right now, though," she added excitedly, "I have a horse to see to!" Pulling her jacket tightly around her, Samantha turned and hurried off to the mares' barn—and Shining!

Yvonne was overjoyed when Samantha told her the news later that morning at school. "Oh, Sammy, that's great! I'm so happy for you. You've done so much for Ashleigh and Mike, I'm glad they appreciate it. Now you'll have even more reason to get Shining healthy again!"

Samantha smiled as she closed her locker door. "I know. I still want to pinch myself to make sure I'm not dreaming."

Yvonne's eyes sparkled. "Hey, maybe you could even get her back to the races again!"

"It would be nice," Samantha said dreamily, "but I

don't want to think that far ahead. I'm afraid to, actually. Right now, I just want to set my goal at getting her fit."

"Yeah," Yvonne agreed, "that's smart."

Tor was happy for Samantha, too, when he called her that night.

"My own horse, Tor!" she told him. "Finally!"

Tor laughed. "I know exactly how you feel, Sammy. I remember when I bought Top Hat—he was the first horse I owned by myself. It was pretty heady." He sobered a little. "Unfortunately, you've got your work cut out for you with Shining."

"I know, but that's okay. She's mine." Privately Samantha had her own doubts and uncertainties about how far she could go with Shining, but she kept them to herself. Positive thinking, that was it.

For several weeks Samantha had few free moments. Early every morning she tumbled out of bed, got dressed, and after swallowing down a quick breakfast, rushed out to the stables. None of the horses remaining at the farm were in active training, but they still had to be groomed, lightly exercised, and put out in the paddocks when weather permitted. In addition to the horses she regularly groomed—Wonder, Fleet Goddess, Sierra, Precocious, Mr. Wonderful, and Shining—Samantha had taken on several of Vic's horses, since he was in Florida with her father. Together she, Len, Mr. Reese, and the two day grooms mucked stalls; filled hay nets, feed mangers, and water buckets; and made sure each horse in the stables had at least a light grooming. In the afternoon, aside from her regular chores, Samantha tried to squeeze in a half-hour visit to Pride at the clinic on her way home from school. He was continuing to improve, which thrilled her. Of course, her hectic schedule didn't leave her as much time as she would have liked to devote to Shining. But whatever free time she had, she spent with the filly, sometimes going out to the barn in the evening, taking her homework with her. Sitting on the bedding in the stall, Samantha would study and give Shining quiet, reassuring company. Samantha felt it was very important that Shining know she was there for her, and the filly seemed to enjoy the attention.

In just the few weeks Shining had been on the farm, she was already showing improvement physically. The worming medication had rid her of parasites, so that the food she ate stayed with her. The hollow spaces between her ribs were slowly filling in. There was a new brightness in her eyes, and with vitamins and Samantha's meticulous grooming, her coat was starting to look healthy. There was still one very large obstacle—teaching Shining that she could trust people again. But Samantha had every intention of overcoming it.

Samantha was already halfway through her senior year at Henry Clay High School, but the worst of her class load had been in the fall. This semester she had only four required classes, with three electives. Back in the fall, she and all her friends had sweated over their latest grades, wanting to have the best GPA possible for their college applications.

Like Ashleigh before her, Samantha had applied to only one school: the University of Kentucky at Lexington. Also like Ashleigh, she planned to study business, farm management, and animal science. It would be at least another month before she heard whether or not she was accepted.

Aside from writing a monthly column on the horse-racing industry for the school newspaper, Samantha had never had time for a lot of extracurricular activities at school, since most of her time was devoted to horses. Last year it seemed every spare moment had been spent with Pride. And because Tor was already out of high school and at the U of K in Lexington, it gave Samantha one less reason to be involved with class activities.

Now, with her father gone, Samantha always rushed right home every afternoon after visiting Pride. Although they didn't have much time to see each other, Samantha talked to Tor every night and shared all the ups and downs of her days. In the last week, she had started to take Shining on long walks while the thin winter light still shone on the hills of Whitebrook. Because the horse didn't have a healthy, thick winter coat, Samantha threw a light horse blanket over Shining's back when they went out. At first they merely walked short distances along the trails at Whitebrook.

After a few days, Len told her that the light exercise seemed to be helping the filly get back some appetite. So, very slowly, they increased her feed, and Samantha started taking her on longer and longer walks. By the weekend they were walking over the trails for two or three miles at a time.

At first Shining seemed reluctant to leave the familiar security of her stall, and it had taken some patient coaxing on Samantha's part to get her outside. Once out, she seemed skittish, shying when Len or Mr. Reese walked up to look at her, and pulling away even from other horses. Out on the trails the least little thing bothered her, from a small branch in the road to a bird twittering overhead. But her behavior only made Samantha more determined and more willing to be patient. After all, Shining was her very own horse.

Slowly, as the days passed, Shining started behaving a little better. When she heard Samantha's footsteps coming toward her stall, she actually put her head over the top to greet her. Samantha was overjoyed. Soon Shining came willingly out of her stall, and though she was still alert and wary, she didn't actually shy from the other horses or from normal outdoor sounds. With every small step of Shining's progress, Samantha felt a rush of pride and hope. If the mare continued to make progress, who knew where she could end up? Maybe she really could go back into training.

More than once Samantha had to snap out of a daydream in which she was standing proudly with Shining in the winner's circle of some race. Shining was draped with a blanket of roses, people were taking their picture, Samantha was modestly giving interviews. . . .

Tor was waiting for Samantha in the stable yard on Friday afternoon when she returned from giving Shining a two-mile walk over the trails. Samantha's and Shining's breath misted in the cool air, but Samantha was smiling. Shining's step was jaunty and her delicate ears were pricked alertly. Most important, she hadn't shied at anything even once during their walk.

Tor hurried over to them with a smile. "I guess it went well," he said. As Samantha stopped Shining, Tor put an arm around Samantha and kissed her forehead. "You have great color in your cheeks."

Samantha smiled up into his blue eyes. "It's good to see you. I've missed you. I'm sorry I've been so busy the past couple of weeks."

"I know you have a lot on your plate," he told her. "You and Len have practically been running this place single-handed. How did you do on that history test?"

"Okay, I think," Samantha said, "but I kind of feel like I'm being run ragged, between all the work here and school—not that I mind work. There's just too much of it! I'll be glad when Dad and the others are back."

Tor laughed. "I'll bet you will. Come on, I'll help you get Shining settled."

Once Shining was back in her stall, Samantha carefully looked her over. The light exercise Samantha had given her hadn't tired her at all, and her coat was free of sweat.

"She looks better," Tor mused, as though surprised. "She's filled out a little, and her muscle tone is coming back." He looked up and gave Samantha a grin. "Samantha 'Miracle-Worker' McLean is doing it again!"

Behind them, Len chuckled. He had come up with Shining's dinner. "That's the truth. This horse has probably never had so much attention in her life." He filled Shining's empty feed bucket. Held in the aisle in her crossties, Shining looked anxiously toward her dinner and nickered softly.

Samantha laughed. "Oh, so you're hungry now, huh? This is a change—a great change." She unclipped Shining's halter and held her while Tor threw a clean light blanket over the horse. Then Shining practically dashed for her stall and buried her nose in her grain.

Surprised, Samantha looked at Tor and Len. Tor was grinning, and Len looked impressed.

"That's the first time I've seen her enthusiastic about her feed," the older man said. "You just might make something of her yet."

"I hope so," Samantha said softly.

That night Samantha and Tor got some takeout Chinese food and brought it back to Whitebrook. Samantha was too exhausted for an actual date.

"You know, we have to put Sierra back into training soon. His shoulder is fine now," Tor said.

Sierra was the big liver-chestnut steeplechaser that Samantha and Tor had been training for the past year.

50

Mike had originally bought the horse to be a flat racer, but when Sierra showed a real affinity for jumping, Samantha had convinced Mike to let her and Tor try him as a 'chaser. After Tor had broken his arm in the spring, Samantha had actually had to ride Sierra in an important steeplechase. Although she had been scared of the 'chase's demanding course, in the end she and Sierra had done very well—much to her astonishment. Last fall, Sierra had pulled a shoulder muscle badly, and they had been forced to take him out of training temporarily.

"Yeah, you're right," Samantha said, then groaned. "How will I find the time? I wish there were two of me."

Tor laughed. "Then I could have one of you all to myself. And the horses could have one of you."

Samantha grinned.

"I'll try to find time to start working him lightly this week," Tor announced, helping himself to some sweet-and-sour pork. "Depending on how he looks and feels, maybe in the spring we can aim him toward that 'chase in Aiken, South Carolina."

Samantha's eyes widened. "That's a big race," she said. "That would so fabulous if he was ready."

Tor nodded. "Speaking of recovering horses, how's Pride?"

Samantha smiled. "I saw him yesterday afternoon at the clinic. He's doing really well. The vet says he can come home soon. I guess we'll wait for Ashleigh and Mike to get back before we pick him up."

"Good news," Tor said.

51

After dinner they watched a rented movie, then Tor, looking at Samantha's sleepy face, decided it was time for him to head home.

"Will you come with me to check the stables one last time?" Samantha asked.

"Sure thing." Tor took her hand.

They walked quickly through the stallion barn, where Mike's four stud horses were all sleeping peacefully, and then through the training stable. Everything was fine there, too, and they both greeted Sierra, who was having a little late-night snack. He stamped one of his front feet when he saw them, as though to say, "Why haven't you taken me out lately?"

In the mares' and young horses' barn, the only sounds were the quiet breathing of contented horses and the occasional swish of straw as a horse shifted in its sleep.

"How's Mr. Wonderful coming along?" Tor asked softly as they came upon his stall.

"Look and see." Samantha waved her hand at the yearling. Wonder's second son was a beautiful honey-colored chestnut, and he had his dam's sweet expression and intelligent eyes. He was very tall and muscular for his age, and altogether quite promising.

"Ash and I can't wait until he begins his training," Samantha whispered as they looked at the dozing colt. "He has tons of potential. Look at those long legs and that straight back. He's really going to be something, I can feel it."

At Shining's stall Samantha pointed silently to her

empty feed manger and grinned at Tor. Shining had retreated to the back of her stall to rest, as she usually did. Was Samantha just imagining it, or did she really look better? She *had* filled out some, hadn't she? Didn't she carry her head higher now? Wasn't there a bit of shine in her eyes?

Samantha sighed. Shining was still a very long way from being a racehorse. She was a long way from being even a *pleasure* horse. Samantha was just going to have to be patient.

Tor turned as Mr. Reese came quietly up the aisle.

"How 'bout a cup of tea before you head out?" he offered Tor.

The three of them went to the farm's small office, where an electric teakettle was already plugged in. All training offices looked alike, Samantha mused, gazing around. The same wooden walls, the same beat-up desks. Photographs of winners, past and present, on the walls. Sometimes a trophy or two. Articles from newspapers clipped out, sometimes framed. She breathed deeply and sat back on the ancient leather couch that smelled of saddle soap and hoof oil. *Someday I would like to have an office like this.*

Five minutes later they were settled with their steaming mugs, listening with quiet contentment to the barely discernible sounds of the stable. One of the stable cats, Sidney, came stalking into the office, brushing his white-and-black body with its odd markings against their legs. A month before, Sidney's mother, Snowshoe, had had her latest litter: a daughter who looked like her, and a son who had the black-

and-white markings of his father, Jeeves. Now the tiny kittens clumsily scampered in after Sidney, mewing excitedly. He gave them a disdainful look as they tumbled around his feet, then tried to ignore them.

Soft footsteps alerted them to Len's arrival. He poked his head into the office and grinned. "Good thing none of us worry too much about the horses," he said dryly.

"There's a cup of tea with your name on it, Len," Mr. Reese said, pouring him a steaming mug. "Take a seat."

Len sat down on a pile of battered horse blankets and took an appreciative sip. "Just got back from seeing Hank, over at Townsend Acres," he said slowly. He and Hank, who was the head groom at the other farm, were old friends.

"Any interesting news?" Samantha asked, brushing a long strand of red hair off her face. Involuntarily her stomach tensed up. It would be fine with her if she never had to think about anything at Townsend Acres again!

"Young Townsend has entered Lord Ainsley in the Santa Anita Handicap in California. Early March. Guess he'll win."

Frowning, Samantha said, "Yeah, he probably will, with Pride out of the way." She tossed her head angrily. In several matches Pride had shown himself to be the better horse, though Lord Ainsley was a gorgeous Thoroughbred with a lot of natural talent. With Pride retired, Lord Ainsley would no doubt eat up the rest of the field.

"Got a look at Her Majesty, that new three-year-old of Lavinia's. Nice-looking horse."

"Terrific bloodlines," Mr. Reese contributed.

"Maybe Lavinia will do us all a favor, and exercise ride her and break her leg," Samantha said snippily, then immediately felt ashamed.

Tor chuckled and made a mewing sound. "I think Sammy's getting cranky."

Samantha couldn't help laughing. "I know that was a horrible thing to say, but it just seems so unfair. Lavinia doesn't know the first thing about horses, but because she has money coming out of her ears, she gets to do anything she wants. Look at what she did to Princess last fall. She wasn't even sorry for the accident—she blamed it on Princess!

"What does it matter if she injured one of the best young horses coming along?" Samantha continued sarcastically. "She can just go out and buy herself another horse whenever she wants. Ooh, I can't stand her!"

Len nodded sympathetically. "At least it looks like they're going to leave Mr. Wonderful here for the time being." Clay Townsend had mentioned keeping the yearling at Townsend Acres to be broken and trained, but so far Ashleigh had been able to talk him out of it.

Sighing, Samantha said, "Yeah. I hope it stays that way. I know Ashleigh's worried about it."

"Only time will tell," Mr. Reese said.

5

ON TUESDAY MORNING SAMANTHA WAS AT HER LOCKER, taking out her books for her morning classes, when Yvonne came up and tapped her on the shoulder. Samantha spun around to see her best friend smiling from ear to ear, her black eyes sparkling.

"Okay, what's up?" Samantha demanded.

"Drum roll, please," Yvonne said dramatically.

Their friend Maureen O'Brien came up in time to hear the last statement. Maureen was the editor of the school paper, the *Henry Clay Herald*. It had been her idea to have Samantha write articles about the local horse industry, including profiles of Wonder's Pride, Sierra, and Fleet Goddess.

Yvonne included Maureen in her excited glance. "Last night," Yvonne said, drawing out the moment, "I bought Cisco!"

"What!" Samantha exclaimed. "You didn't tell you'd saved enough. Tor never said a word to me either."

"I told him not to say anything until I told you," Yvonne responded. "Tor and I worked out a deal. I still owe him some more money, which I'll pay off little by little. But he sold Cisco for a really good price. Now we *both* own our own horses, Sammy!" Yvonne was practically bouncing up and down with excitement.

"That's terrific!" Maureen said. "I can't believe it. Cisco is really beautiful, and you guys make such a good team. I'm so happy for you."

Yvonne beamed. "Thanks."

Samantha leaned over and hugged Yvonne. "That is great news, Yvonne. Now you'll be riding your own horse when you compete in the National Horse Show."

Yvonne nodded, but her smile slipped a little.

"What's wrong?" Samantha asked, putting her book bag over her shoulder. The three girls started down the hall to their first classes.

Yvonne swallowed. "I feel a little nervous about competing," she admitted.

"Why?" Maureen asked. "You were so excited about being accepted, and you and Cisco are doing so well."

"And anyway," Samantha said, putting her hand on Yvonne's arm, "you're only entering the novice division. It doesn't matter if you don't win. It'll be an incredible experience for you. You know they never would have accepted you if you weren't one of the top jumpers your age in the country. And since you're seventeen, you have only two years left of junior competition."

The girls edged closer as students began to stream past them into the classroom.

"You're right. I just wish Tor and Top Hat were competing, too," Yvonne said, wrinkling her nose. "I'd feel better."

"Tor doesn't think they'll be ready, since they lost so much training time after he broke his arm. But he'll be there with you as your coach," Samantha said encouragingly.

"That's true," Yvonne said, looking a little brighter. "I guess it'll be okay."

"Of course it will," Samantha said firmly.

One afternoon, Samantha gave Shining a long jog along the trails of Whitebrook, picking up their pace to a trot. Shining seemed to love it. It was the first week of February and the temperature had warmed up a tiny bit, so Shining didn't have to wear a blanket.

Finally Samantha huffed to a stop so they could walk awhile. "More for my benefit than yours, girl," she admitted, her panting breaths making sharp puffs of steam in the air. They walked in companionable silence for several long minutes, with Samantha watching Shining's every move. The filly had a nice, easy gait, both at a walk and a trot. It was a good sign.

"Shining," Samantha said, "how do you feel about starting on a longe line soon? Maybe next weekend? I'd like to see how you canter."

Shining whoofed loudly, bobbing her head.

"Okay, then. We'll do it."

Lately, Shining had seemed more interested in her

surroundings on their walks. When birds flew by, she tracked them with her eyes, she stepped carefully over small branches in her way, and she looked at other horses with interest, her elegant nose sniffing the air to catch their scent. In the past few days, Samantha thought the filly even picked up her feet more when she trotted, making her look more energetic and enthusiastic.

"Are you getting used to us, girl?" Samantha asked softly, resting her head against Shining's warm neck. "Have you started to realize that no one here will hurt you? That we all just wish you well and want you to be happy? I know you could be really special. And just between you and me, I really want you to go into training."

Shining walked along, every once in a while turning to look at Samantha, as though the sound of Samantha's voice calmed her—was special to her. Samantha reached forward and gently rubbed Shining's soft, clean nose. It was like chilly velvet under her fingers. "I want you to race again," Samantha whispered. "But only if you want to."

Samantha headed back toward home. She still had to remind herself that they had a long way to go and it was too early to get her hopes up for Shining's return to the racetrack.

That evening Samantha stood tiredly in front of the refrigerator, wondering what she could have for dinner. She sighed. Looked like another frozen meal. Since her father had been gone, she hadn't bothered much with cooking. Tor had rescued her several times, and often she ate with Len or Mr. Reese or both, but tonight she was on her own. And she felt completely uninspired.

The doorbell interrupted her examination of the freezer.

"Beth! This is a surprise," Samantha said, pulling open the door.

"Well, I'm flying down to Florida tomorrow to see Blues King race," Beth said. "So I thought I would drop by tonight. I brought you this." She thrust a foil-covered casserole dish at Samantha.

"What is it?" Samantha asked, motioning Beth in.

Beth dropped her purse on the couch. "Oh, just a vegetable casserole," she said. She followed Samantha into the kitchen. "I thought maybe I could stay and help you eat it."

"Great," Samantha said cheerfully. "I was just wondering what to fix for dinner. While this is heating, I'll throw together a salad."

Half an hour later they were seated at the kitchen table, and Samantha was eating ravenously. She hadn't realized how hungry she was.

"Have you been eating properly, Sammy?" Beth asked with concern.

Nodding, Samantha laughed. "I have been, I promise. I'm just starving today after working with Shining."

"Oh, good." Beth looked relieved. "Has everything been going okay, since your dad's been gone?" she asked casually.

"Uh-huh." Samantha took another bite of the

61

casserole. "It's just been really busy, since Len and Mr. Reese and I are doing all the work ourselves. I'll be glad when everyone's back."

"I'm really excited about going down tomorrow. Races must seem like old hat to you, but I haven't seen many, and they're still a big thrill for me."

Smiling, Samantha said, "Oh, they're still a thrill for me, too. Especially when I know one of the horses running."

"I'll be sad to miss the Pony Commandos on Sunday—be sure to give them my love. They're really coming along well, aren't they?"

Samantha nodded. "I bet they would come to class every day if they could. But every other week is about all Tor and I can manage. I just adore Mandy Jarvis—she has so much courage and determination. A few weeks ago she told me her dream is to ride racehorses." She smiled at the memory.

"She's terrific," Beth agreed. "And how about you? Are you sure you haven't been too lonesome here on your own? You're okay with money and everything, right?" Beth looked at her plate, suddenly seeming embarrassed.

Samantha looked at her quizzically. Why was Beth asking so many questions? It wasn't like her. "I'm fine, Beth."

"Okay, I admit it!" Beth cried. "I'm no good at this. I told him so." She rested her forehead on her hand.

"Beth, what are you talking about?" Samantha asked, thoroughly mystified.

"It was your father," Beth said, spilling the beans.

"He wanted me come over here to see if you were coping okay. I fixed the casserole as an excuse." She looked totally mortified. "I would have come over anyway—just to visit."

Samantha stared at her for a moment, then burst out laughing. "But I talk to Dad every night!" she exclaimed. "I would have told him if anything was wrong."

"I know, I know," Beth said. "That's what I told him, too. But I think he's having a hard time accepting the fact that you're a young woman, and not a little girl anymore." She let out a long breath of relief. "At least now I can fly down to Florida and report that you're eating, sleeping, and changing your clothes every day."

She and Samantha laughed.

Samantha and Tor vanned Sierra over to Tor's stable as soon as Samantha had finished her morning chores. The turf track at Whitebrook was still muddy and frozen, so they were going to use Tor's inside ring. Smiling, Samantha told him about Beth's visit of the night before.

"Well, at least Ashleigh and Mike will be home in about a week," she said. "Then Dad can quit worrying."

First Samantha warmed up Sierra at a trot and a canter, twice around the indoor ring. Then she handed the reins over to Tor, and he put the big horse through some simple jumps. Standing at the side, Samantha watched admiringly as Tor effortlessly guided Sierra through a modified course over several brush jumps.

He went through the course twice easily. Samantha knew that Sierra was capable of jumping much higher and more difficult props, but this was his first real workout since he had pulled his shoulder muscle, and it was sensible for Tor to take it easy.

"Nice," Samantha applauded when Tor circled the big horse back to her. "Very nice. How did he feel?"

"He felt great!" Tor said, dismounting. "As though he hasn't missed any training at all. He loves to jump, don't you, boy?" He rubbed the chestnut's neck firmly.

Sierra tossed his head and gave a little sideways prance.

Samantha laughed. "Right, you monster," she said, affectionately patting his rump. "I guess you deserve some praise for that workout. If only you weren't so sure of it!"

"I really think he might be ready in time for the Aiken 'chase," Tor said excitedly. "I'm just wondering about my own schedule." Tor paused for a moment, thinking. Samantha knew he had to take into account the jumping classes he taught, his college courses, training Top Hat, seeing her . . .

"How long do you think we need to condition him before he's in top shape again?" Samantha asked.

"A month and a half, at least." Brushing back his blond hair, Tor said, "But I figure maybe we can manage it." He looked up at Sierra and grinned. "This big guy deserves the chance to win some 'chases. I say we do it. We'll find the time somehow. We always have before. And as soon as Ashleigh and Mike are back, your schedule will lighten up a lot."

They slapped high fives. "Let's do it!" Samantha cried.

After Sierra had been handed off to a groom for cooling down, Samantha helped Tor set up the ring for the Pony Commandos, who would have their lesson the next morning. White-painted beams called cavallettis were placed at regular intervals flat on the ground. These were used to train both horses and riders in the very early stages of learning to jump. The kids would enjoy stepping their ponies over them, Samantha knew.

"Oh, Sammy, I've been thinking," Tor said, shifting one of the large double jumps out of the way. "You know how much Mandy Jarvis loves horses, right?"

"I sure do," Samantha replied. "It's all she talks about."

"Well, then, how about taking her to Whitebrook someday to see Shining? She could see some of the other horses, too. I bet she'd love it."

Samantha stopped in her tracks. "Tor, that's a great idea! Why didn't I think of that? I would love to show her Whitebrook. I'll ask her parents tomorrow at class," she said excitedly. She went over to Tor and threw her arms around him. "That must be why I'm so crazy about you. You're always thinking of other people."

Tor put his arms around her and drew her close for a long, lingering kiss. "I'm always thinking about *you*, anyway," he murmured.

"I'm always thinking about you, too," Samantha

said back softly. Then she smiled. "And Shining, and Wonder, and Mr. Wonderful, and my father, my school, and Yvonne, and Precocious, and . . ."

She dissolved into giggles as Tor, pretending mock outrage, began tickling her, chasing her all around the ring.

6

THE FOLLOWING SATURDAY, SAMANTHA TOOK SHINING FOR a long jog early in the morning. The filly now kept pace with her easily, and seemed to enjoy their outings. Though it was only the second week of February, the weather had been exceptionally mild and dry, and most of the snow had melted. Tiny purple and yellow crocuses and snowdrops had pushed determinedly through the cold soil, and now nodded in the breeze.

"Well, Shining," Samantha panted as they walked toward home, "Ashleigh and Mike will be back tomorrow. I wonder if they'll see an improvement in you. You've been here a month now."

As if in response, Shining bobbed her head on the long lead, whoofing out her breath.

"Oh, you think so? Remember, I was going to try the longe line tomorrow." Samantha patted the horse's neck as they turned into the stable yard. Then they walked up and down for several minutes while Shining cooled out and her breathing returned to normal.

"She's looking good," Len called, coming up to them. When he reached Shining, she looked at him expectantly, then lowered her finely boned head to sniff at his pockets.

"Len!" Samantha said, pretending to be shocked. "Shining looks as though she's waiting for you to give her a treat. She's beginning to trust you."

Len pulled out a piece of broken carrot and let the horse lip it delicately from his weathered hand. "Really? That's nice, Sammy," he said innocently as Shining crunched her carrot.

Laughing, Samantha said, "Just as an educated guess, I'd say you've been sneaking her carrots."

Len grinned and rubbed his hand along the filly's neck. "Maybe. I'm not admitting anything. But she does seem to be less skittish around me."

"It's bribery, and you know it. Now, would you do me a favor and get her settled in her stall? Today's the day I'm bringing Mandy Jarvis over to see her, and I've got to run to Lexington to pick her up."

"Sure thing, Sammy. Come on, Shining girl."

Mandy and her parents lived in an elegant two-story brick house in one of the nicer suburbs of Lexington. Samantha found the address easily.

Even before she had a chance to ring the doorbell, the door opened and Mandy stood there, leaning on her crutches, a huge smile on her face.

"Hi, Sammy!" she cried. "I've been waiting for you!"

"I see that," Samantha replied with a grin.

Mr. and Mrs. Jarvis were right behind Mandy, and they shook Samantha's hand.

"I can't tell you how excited Mandy is about visiting your stable," Mrs. Jarvis said, a smile lighting her pretty face. "She could hardly sleep last night."

"We really appreciate your interest in our little fighter," Mr. Jarvis said, placing an affectionate hand on his daughter's shoulder.

"Well, I'm very excited about showing Whitebrook to Mandy. She's a natural with horses," Samantha replied.

Thirty minutes later Samantha parked her father's car in front of the McLean cottage. "This is where my father and I live," she said, pointing. "And over there is where Ashleigh, Mike, and Mike's father live. Remember, I told you Ashleigh is co-owner of Wonder's Pride and several other horses."

"I remember. She came to our Christmas party." Mandy's large, coffee-brown eyes were darting here and there, trying to take in everything at once. "It's beautiful here," she said. "I want to see the whole place! I don't even know where to start."

Samantha smiled and helped the little girl out of the car. Heavy leg braces kept her thin limbs steady, and Mandy was adept at getting around on her short metal crutches. Samantha made a mental note to herself not to let Mandy overdo it.

"I thought first we should see Shining, my horse—the one I told you about," Samantha suggested, leading Mandy slowly to the mares' barn. On the way she pointed out the other two barns and explained their uses, promising a tour later. Mandy looked at the large outdoor training ring with awe.

"That's so much bigger than Tor's ring!" she exclaimed. "Is that where you train your horses?"

"Yep. See, Mr. Reese is out there now, working one of his horses."

They waved to him, and he waved cheerfully back.

When they reached the mares' barn, they met Len coming out, and Samantha made the introductions.

Solemnly, Len reached down to shake hands. "So you like horses, do you?" he asked.

"I love them!" Mandy declared, her face glowing.

"And do you like kittens? We have some kittens, too."

"Really? Can I see them?" Mandy asked eagerly.

"Right this way, young lady."

The three of them walked down the main aisle to Shining's stall. Samantha was surprised to see Snowshoe and her two new kittens playing right outside the filly's stall. Even more surprising was that Shining had poked her head over the top and was looking at the exuberant kittens with what seemed like amused patience. Under their mother's watchful eye, the small tiger-striped female and almost solid-black male were practicing their stall-climbing techniques.

Laughing with delight, Mandy settled herself on a hay bale by the wall and watched the kittens trying to scale the wooden stall partition. Then, noticing that they had company, the kittens scampered over to Mandy and fearlessly leaped up on the hay bale to examine her.

"They're so cute," Mandy said wonderingly as the small kittens sniffed her eagerly and climbed into her lap. "What are their names?"

Len looked surprised. "You know, I don't think anyone has gotten around to naming them yet. Things have been kind of busy around here. Maybe you should pick out some nice names for them."

Mandy turned glowing eyes to Len. "Could I?" she squealed, petting the kittens gently. "Really?"

"Really," Samantha assured her, dropping to her knees so she'd be at Mandy's eye level. "Think of some good ones. Their mother's name is Snowshoe, if that helps any."

For several long moments Mandy regarded the kittens thoughtfully, her small forehead creased in concentration.

"Okay," she said finally, picking up the gray kitten. "Your name will be Flurry 'cause you're gray, like a snow flurry."

"That's a great name," Samantha said approvingly.

"And you . . ." Mandy picked up the black kitten, who gently tapped her cheek with one velvet paw. "I think I'll call you Midnight."

"Those are two terrific names," Samantha said. "Flurry and Midnight it is."

"Now can I meet Shining, and the other horses?" Mandy asked eagerly.

"Sure can."

The kittens tumbled off Mandy's lap, and with a last, loving pat she let them scamper away. Then she gathered her crutches and stood to make her way to

Shining's stall door. Samantha pushed open the half-door, and Shining came forward, her previous shyness forgotten for a moment. Curiously she leaned her head down over the chain across the opening.

Watching Mandy tenderly reach up one small hand to pet Shining, Samantha felt a rush of surprise at Shining's response. Although the filly had gotten used to her, Len, and even Mr. Reese, she was still definitely wary of strangers. When the farrier, Tamara Wilson, had come to put new shoes on her feet, it had taken all of Samantha's strength to hold her in place and keep her still.

"Hello, Shining," Mandy was crooning. "You're so pretty. You're the prettiest horse I've ever seen."

Shining carefully lowered her head farther so Mandy could rub higher on her face, almost up to her ears. Above Mandy's head, Samantha met Len's eyes. His eyebrows were raised.

"Sammy told me you had been sick," Mandy was saying very softly. Her small head, with its cap of silky black curls, reached barely halfway up Shining's shoulder. But the horse seemed to listen patiently to her young visitor.

"I've been sick, too," Mandy said in practically a whisper. "I was in the hospital a long time." She looked down at her braces. "Now I have to wear these clunky things. All I want to do is run again. And ride horses." She rested her forehead against the fine, soft hairs on Shining's muzzle. Samantha held her breath, but Shining seemed completely at ease. "Do you want to run, Shining?" Mandy asked. "I bet you could run so fast. Someday I'll have to come see you run." Her tiny hand still on Shining's nose, Mandy asked Samantha, "Do you ride her?"

"Not yet," Samantha replied, swallowing the lump in her throat that the tender scene had caused. "I wanted to wait until she's a little stronger. But I think I'll start training her again soon, and then we'll know what she can do."

Mandy stepped back awkwardly, with Shining watching her intently. "Can I come see her again?"

"You bet. She really likes you, I can tell. She doesn't let many people get that close to her." Samantha smiled gently at the little girl. "You're good for her, Mandy."

Mandy sighed happily. "She's good for me, too, Sammy."

"And then Len picked up Mandy and we finished the tour of Whitebrook with her riding his shoulders," Samantha told Tor, Yvonne, and Gregg that night. Since Ashleigh and Mike were due home the next day, Samantha had invited her friends over for dinner on her last night alone. The four of them, amid much laughter and goofing around, had managed to put together a simple meal of spaghetti, salad, and bread.

"She's a real trooper," Tor said admiringly, helping himself to more salad.

"She's a good rider, too," Yvonne said. "When is she supposed to get the braces off?"

Samantha frowned. "I'm not sure. I think her

73

parents are afraid she might not ever be able to walk totally unaided. But they did tell me that she's improved a lot since she started riding with the Pony Commandos. She's happier, so her attitude is better, and she's doing everything the doctors are telling her. Her special exercises and stuff."

"That's great," Gregg said, putting an arm around Yvonne's shoulders.

"The weird thing was how Shining reacted to her. It was like they were old friends. Shining has never been so calm or friendly around a stranger before."

"Maybe Shining could sense that Mandy has had a hard time, just like her," Yvonne suggested seriously. "Maybe she could recognize a kindred spirit."

"You might be right," Samantha mused, breaking off a piece of bread. "They looked so great together. I'm definitely going to bring Mandy back soon. Now," she said, her face brightening, "let's talk about our plans for the Sadie Hawkins dance at school. Do you guys want to have dinner together before?"

"Yeah, let's," Gregg agreed, pretending great interest in the discussion. "Tor, what are you going to wear?"

The girls started breaking up with laughter as Tor said thoughtfully, "I don't know, Gregg. I was thinking of my mauve, or perhaps the emerald green."

Samantha punched him on the shoulder. "Idiot. You don't even know what color mauve is!"

Early on Sunday morning, Samantha, Len, and even Mr. Reese ran around like crazy, mucking out stalls, polishing tack, and sprucing up every horse to look his or her best, all in preparation for Ashleigh and Mike's return. Last night Tor had helped Samantha make a big Welcome Home sign, and now it hung prominently above the front door on the main farmhouse.

Pausing for a minute from sweeping out the main aisle of the mares' barn, Samantha stopped to double-check that every horse looked in tip-top shape.

"Hello, Wonder," she said, affectionately patting the chestnut's nose. "Your favorite person will be home soon, and I bet she can't wait to see you. And you, Fleet Goddess—you look like you're carrying twins! I know you've been waiting for Ashleigh and Mike to get home, but I think you can relax and have your baby now."

The two yearlings, Mr. Wonderful and Precocious, trotted anxiously up to the stall doors as Samantha walked by. They seemed to have picked up on the sense of urgency in the air, and Samantha took the time to stroke them soothingly and give them pieces of carrot from the bin.

"And finally Shining," Samantha said softly. "My beautiful Shining. I can't wait to show Ashleigh how much difference three weeks has made!" Shining obediently came forward and let Samantha pet her nose and muzzle.

The sound of a car's horn tooting up the drive made Samantha start. "Oh, my gosh," she gasped. "They're here!" She ran out to the stable yard, calling to Len and Mr. Reese.

"They're here! They're back!"

A minute later Ashleigh and Mike had stepped from the taxi, and the driver was unloading all their bags. Samantha found herself enveloped in a warm hug from Ashleigh, and then Mike.

"You're so tan!" Samantha exclaimed, looking them both over. A rush of happiness coursed through her, and she realized that she had missed her two friends more than she had expected.

After everyone had hugged and shaken hands and commented on how fit and tan Ashleigh and Mike looked, Ashleigh suddenly spun in a circle, taking in her surroundings as though she'd never seen them before.

"Oh! It's good to be back!" she cried, her hazel eyes gazing around the farm. Samantha followed her gaze and saw Whitebrook as though for the first time: rolling hills, still dotted here and there with snow, white-painted rail fences, oak trees, bare sycamores, and black pines covered with sweet-smelling needles. The stable yard was large and tidy, swept clean and with its equipment organized neatly. The barns were kept in meticulous repair and were painted the traditional brick-red color, which had been softened a bit by the elements. The farmhouse and the two smaller cottages were all painted a crisp white and had stone walkways leading to the main driveway.

Ashleigh looked over and caught Samantha's eye. "It's good to be back," she said again. "Though we had a great time—we have tons of pictures to show everyone. And presents!"

"Now don't tell me—let me guess what you want to do first before we even unpack," Mike teased Ashleigh gently.

"Go see the horses!" everyone cried.

In the mares' barn, Ashleigh looked at Fleet Goddess with a practiced eye. "I was sure she'd have foaled by now," she murmured. "Looks like it could happen any minute."

Samantha followed Ashleigh happily through the tour of the stables, pointing out how Mr. Wonderful and Precocious had grown, informing her and Mike of the new kittens' names.

"Oh, Mike—guess what? Dad called last night, and Blues King won at Gulfstream yesterday," Samantha informed him.

"All right!" Mike exclaimed. "I knew he'd come through for us—he's the only hope we have racing this year."

"Wonder! Hey, girl," Ashleigh cried, hurrying to the chestnut's stall and throwing her arms around Wonder's neck. "How's my girl? You look very good, yes, you do. Oh, I missed you." Ashleigh turned back to everyone with a smile. "Mike was teasing me about missing the horses so much. He said next time we go on vacation we have to find a place where we can bring Wonder with us."

Samantha laughed. "You'll need an extra-big room."

"Sammy and I have been going to see Pride regularly, you know," Len said. "Dr. Mendez says he'll be ready to come home in a few weeks. They just want to make sure he's totally healed."

"That's good," Ashleigh said. "I'll go see him to-morrow."

"I'll go with you," Mike offered.

They had been progressing steadily toward Shining's stall, and Samantha's heart was in her throat. *She* thought the filly looked better, but what if she was wrong—just kidding herself? Ashleigh and Mike had given her a huge responsibility when they'd signed over Shining's papers to her. She had to show them that they had done the right thing.

"And here's Shining," she said faintly as they approached the filly's stall.

Shining, hearing many different footsteps, was hanging back in the rear of her stall. Samantha knew crowds made her uneasy. Stepping in front of Len and Mr. Reese, Samantha put her hand over Shining's stall door.

"Hey, sweetie," she said softly. "It's just me. Come show Ashleigh and Mike how you look."

Shining's ears pricked alertly at the sound of Samantha's voice, and trustingly she stepped forward. Coming to the stall door, she nudged Samantha's hand with her nose, then butted her shoulder softly. Samantha was thrilled. It was the most affection the filly had shown her yet.

Both Ashleigh and Mike stepped closer to examine Shining.

"Wow, Sammy, I can't believe this is the same horse," Ashleigh said softly, trying not to startle Shining. Gently she reached out a hand and rubbed Shining's muzzle. "She looks one hundred percent better."

"Really?" Samantha felt incredibly pleased.

"She really does," Mike confirmed. "It's clear she's still a little skittish, but her looks have sure improved. She's filled out, her coat looks better, she looks livelier, brighter. You've done great with her so far."

"Have you started training her at all?" Ashleigh asked.

Samantha shook her head. "No. We go for long jogs, but I was waiting till you came home before I put her on a longe line."

"I can actually believe she's Wonder's half-sister now," Ashleigh said, running her hand gently along the filly's nose. "Her beauty and conformation are beginning to show."

"She has a nice smooth gait, too," Samantha said.

Ashleigh continued to rub the horse's head, crooning softly to her. "I was thinking about her while we were away," Ashleigh said. "Thinking about her racing again. Mike says we shouldn't get our hopes up— she didn't win anything even racing on second-rate tracks."

"That might have had something to do with how she was being treated," Samantha said with a touch of anger. She still couldn't fathom how anyone had let such a beautiful horse get into such bad shape.

"I know. Wouldn't it be something if she has even a little of Wonder's talent?" Ashleigh said wistfully.

"Yeah, it would," Samantha agreed quietly.

7

"HOW'S IT GOING?" ASHLEIGH CALLED OVER THE FENCE the next morning.

In the yearling training ring, Samantha was circling Shining on the end of a longe line.

Sighing, Samantha brushed a wisp of hair off her forehead. "Let's just say that 'good' would be an overstatement." A twinge of frustration wrinkled her brow. She had been trying to work Shining on the longe line, but getting nowhere. The filly seemed to have absolutely no clue as to what Samantha wanted. Knowing that her own feelings and attitude would be picked up immediately by Shining, Samantha was trying to keep her impatience firmly in check. But it was getting harder.

Ashleigh stepped through the wide rails of the fence and came over to stand by Samantha.

"What's the problem?"

Samantha frowned. "It's weird. She just isn't

responding. Look at her—she seems completely puzzled as to why we're here, and why she's on a long lead."

"Has she responded to any of your signals?" Ashleigh asked. Samantha knew that the clicks, hand motions, and words she had been using on Shining were pretty much standard throughout the horse world.

Samantha shook her head. "Nope. It's as though no one has ever worked her on a longe line before. She should have learned all this in yearling training before she ever went out on a racecourse."

Putting a horse through its paces at the end of a longe line was a key element of training. The controlled environment strengthened the bond between horse and trainer, and by closely watching the horse circle around the ring, a trainer could learn the characteristics of a horse's gait and work on correcting any flaws or problems.

"Let me see," Ashleigh said.

So once again Samantha clicked her tongue and gently snapped a whip in the air behind Shining. The filly jumped forward a bit, then turned and looked at Samantha as if to say, "What in the world are you doing?"

Even Samantha, as frustrated as she was, couldn't help laughing at the horse's quizzical expression.

"You're right," Ashleigh said with a frown. "She doesn't know what you want her to do. I'm sorry, Sammy, but to me it looks like you're going to have to go back to square one and begin Shining's training all over again, as though she were a yearling who had just been broken."

"That's what I was figuring, too." Samantha shook her head, then walked over and patted Shining's neck. "Poor girl. No wonder you didn't win any races. Whoever trained you sure made a mess of it. But we'll just take it nice and slow, and do it right this time, okay?"

Shining whoofed softly as though to say, "I'm game."

Laughing, Ashleigh said, "What a sweetheart she is. It's just a shame that I've given you a bigger project than either of us expected."

"That's okay," Samantha said quickly, looking at Shining. "I don't mind. After all, she's my girl, aren't you, Shining?" She dropped a kiss on the filly's neck, and Shining gave her a shy, pleased look.

"Hmm, let me have a sip," Tor said, putting his arm around Samantha. They were standing at the side of the big indoor ring at Tor's stable, watching Yvonne and Cisco run through a practice session. Only two and a half weeks remained until the National Horse Show at the beginning of March.

Wordlessly Samantha handed Tor her Diet Coke, keeping her eyes on Yvonne. Yvonne and Cisco expertly cleared a large double brush jump, then circled around to take a five-foot gate, a two-fence combination, and a wide parallel jump. With a familiarity born of long hours of practice, Cisco responded to Yvonne's commands almost before she gave them.

"Keep him collected," Tor muttered as they circled the ring. As though she could hear him, Yvonne gathered the reins slightly and checked Cisco before his stride lengthened too much. By keeping his stride collected, she paced him perfectly for the last series of jumps, and they approached the first one at exactly the right speed and momentum.

"Yes!" Samantha said, watching as her friend sailed over the three jumps in a row. "Wow—she looks great, doesn't she? I can't believe that two years ago she had never jumped at all."

"Yeah—she's really talented. She has an instinct and a feel for it, and she knows how to read Cisco's movements and emotions. They're a great team."

"It was good of you to let her have Cisco before she had all the money together," Samantha said, leaning her head on Tor's shoulder.

Cracking a grin, Tor admitted, "She's working off the rest of what she owes. If I play my cards right, I won't have to muck out another stall until I'm about thirty-five."

"Oh, you!" Samantha punched him playfully.

Yvonne posted Cisco to a stop in front of her friends.

"How'd we do?" she asked with a frown.

"Fabulous, and you know it," Samantha said firmly.

"You really did look good out there. You two are definitely ready for the National Horse Show," Tor told her.

For a moment a cloud passed over Yvonne's face,

and she swung down out of Cisco's saddle and played with his bridle, unable to meet Samantha's eyes.

"What is it, Yvonne?" Samantha knew her friend too well. Something was up.

"I'm not going," Yvonne mumbled, looking down at the toes of her boots.

"What?" Samantha cried. Tor laid a hand on her back, sending a silent signal.

"I know you think I'm a big ninny," Yvonne said. "And maybe I am. All I know is that it's one thing to enter meets around here, and something else entirely to enter the National Horse Show at the Meadowlands! I just can't do it. What if I fall? What if I humiliate myself in front of thousands of people? I just can't do it. I'll have to forfeit my entry fee."

"Yvonne," Tor said calmly, "I understand that you're very nervous. I'd be surprised if you weren't. But just think about it. You and Cisco are a perfectly matched team, and you've both had competition experience. In fact, it's because you've done so well in other competitions that you're qualified to enter the NHS. And if you compete in this show, you'll be up against some of the same people you've beaten in other shows." His blue eyes looked at her earnestly. "You're jumping in novice. The other riders are all at basically the same level as you. True, your audience will be bigger than ever before, but you and Cisco have worked hard for this. I believe you can do it. Sammy and Gregg believe it. If you're going to be a serious competitor—and that's what you've always told me you want to be—then you have to overcome your fears. You have to get out there and take the risk."

Yvonne frowned. "So, in other words, I'm just a chicken."

"I'm not saying that," Tor said. "No one would ever look down on you for having natural fears. Don't you think I feel nervous and more than a little scared every time Top Hat and I go into the show ring? Of course I do. And so do most of the other riders. It's normal. What you have to do is believe in yourself enough to put those fears aside."

Yvonne looked down and heaved a huge sigh. When she looked up, there was a rueful smile on her lips. "I think I get the message," she said with a touch of her good humor returning. "I'd be an absolute dope to back out now after I've come this far. I wouldn't only be letting myself down, I'd be letting you and Cisco down, too. All right! You win! I'm going!"

"Yes!" Samantha cheered, punching her fist in the air. "Atta girl!" She hurried over to give her friend a hug.

"I'll tell you what," Tor said with a grin. "I'll sweeten the deal—dinner and a Broadway show in New York—that is, as long as you don't back out again."

Yvonne turned to look at Cisco. He bobbed his head, then gently lipped the brim of her hat. Yvonne laughed. "Cisco seems to think I should agree. It's a deal—but I get to choose the restaurant *and* the show."

Tor grinned. "Sure, and you'll probably put me in the poorhouse in the process."

A chill wind whipped lacy tendrils of red hair against Samantha's cheek as she galloped Rocky Heights, the gray gelding Mike had bought along with Shining, along the backstretch of the Whitebrook training oval on Tuesday morning. Now that Mike and Ashleigh were back, training was in full swing again. Nearly two months of good food and loving treatment had done wonders for the three-year-old, too, and Rocky was looking more and more as if he had real potential.

Coming out of the far turn, Samantha kneaded her hands up Rocky's neck, urging him into a full-blown gallop as they breezed out the last two furlongs. The gelding was responding nicely, and Samantha thought this was a horse that showed real promise.

As they whipped past the mile marker pole, Samantha stood in her stirrups and gradually drew Rocky back into a canter, then a trot, before turning him and heading back to the gap, where Mike, Ashleigh, and Mandy Jarvis were waiting. Mandy's parents had brought the girl over early that morning to watch the workouts.

"Decent!" Mike said with a smile as Samantha rode off the oval and stopped beside them. "I think he'll be ready to go to the races this spring." As Samantha dismounted, Mike checked over the gelding. Samantha looked at Mandy.

"So what did you think?" she asked.

Mandy's sparkling eyes were the only answer she needed. "Someday *I'm* going to ride like that! Wow!"

Samantha chuckled and handed Rocky's reins to Len, who had come to collect him and cool him out. "Nice job, Rocky. Good boy!" Len congratulated.

The gelding bobbed his head and whinnied.

Mandy laughed with delight. "He said he knows!" she cried, clapping her mittened hands together.

"You should see Ashleigh ride. She's a professional jockey," Samantha said.

Mandy turned wide brown eyes on Ashleigh. "I know. My daddy reads about her in the newspaper." Mandy turned back to Samantha. "Are you going to ride more horses now?"

"Sorry, not this morning," Samantha said, lifting Mandy off the stool and setting her down on the ground. "Mike's other horses are still in Florida, and Pride is at the clinic in Lexington. But let's go see Shining, okay? She's been asking about you."

Matching her pace to the little girl's, Samantha started to lead the way toward the mares' barn. As soon as they entered they ran into Mr. and Mrs. Jarvis, finishing up their tour of Whitebrook with Mr. Reese.

"I can see why you love it here, Mandy," Mr. Jarvis said, a smile lighting his face as he looked at his daughter. "Whitebrook is charming. I had no idea horse breeding could be so fascinating."

"Have you seen Shining yet? She's Sammy's own horse," Mandy said. "The one I told you about."

"Please show us," Mrs. Jarvis requested, resting a hand on Mandy's shoulder.

Mandy was the first to reach Shining's stall, and hearing her voice, Shining immediately came forward and put her head over the door.

"Hi, Shining!" Mandy said eagerly. "Look, Mama. Isn't she beautiful?"

Though Shining did look much better than she had when she arrived, Samantha knew that the filly still had a long way to go before she could be called beautiful. Or at least, beautiful to anyone who didn't love her.

"She's very nice," Mrs. Jarvis said diplomatically.

Once again, Shining responded unusually well to Mandy's soft voice and gentle touch. She lowered her head and blew sweet-smelling breath at Mandy, making the little girl giggle.

"Have you ridden her yet?" Mandy asked Samantha.

"Not yet, but she's back in training."

"Maybe you could ride her soon," Mandy said, stroking Shining's velvety nose. As if sensing Mandy's desire, Shining dropped her head even lower. With a delighted smile Mandy stretched up her arms and wrapped them around Shining's neck. "Oh, Shining, you're so beautiful. You're the most beautiful horse in the world!"

Patiently the filly stood as Mandy hugged her, seeming to sense that any sudden movement might make the little girl topple off balance.

When Mandy turned back to Samantha and her parents, Samantha said, "Well, you've worked your magic again, Mandy. Shining never seems so happy as when she's visiting with you."

Mandy's small face split into a beaming smile. "She's feeling better now, Sammy. I think she's ready to run again—like I will be someday. I'm doing really good at my riding at Tor's stable, aren't I?"

"You sure are," Samantha said firmly, swallowing her fears about the little girl's full recovery. "You're just about the best Pony Commando there is."

Mandy turned her beaming face to her parents, who looked proud and pleased.

After Mandy had been settled comfortably in the backseat of her parents' car, Mrs. Jarvis turned a grateful look to Samantha.

"We can't thank you enough for all you've done for Mandy," she said. "She loves her visits here, and she's made so much progress since she's started her riding lessons with Tor. I really think you and your friends have made the difference between a successful recovery and being dependent on crutches."

"I enjoy every minute with Mandy," Samantha assured her. "She's a special little girl. And she really is a good rider—physically challenged or not."

Mandy's parents gave pleased smiles. "Well, thank you again. You and Shining mean a lot to her—and to us."

The following Sunday the Pony Commandos trotted over cavallettis for the first time. Samantha led Butterball and Mandy over them, noting how straight the little girl kept her back, and how much concentration was etched on her determined face.

"Well done!" she praised Mandy afterward, then

turned to the rest of the class. "You all did really well. We'll have you jumping the four-foot brush jump in no time!" With a grin she motioned over to the large jump that was pushed against the rail, out of the way. The Pony Commandos laughed. They knew that even experienced and older riders would train for a long time before attempting such a jump.

"I bet I'll do it someday," Mandy declared. "I bet I will!"

Samantha patted Mandy's shoulder affectionately. "I bet you will, too, sweetie."

"How's Shining?" Mandy asked eagerly as Samantha helped her down from Butterball's saddle.

"You saw her only two days ago," Samantha said, laughing. "But actually, I do have news. Yesterday, for the first time, she worked well on the longe line."

"Really?" Mandy's dark eyes were round with excitement.

"Uh-huh. She went around perfectly at a walk, then a trot, then a canter, all on my command. I think she's smart—she just hasn't been given a chance to prove it."

"When will you ride her?" Mandy asked breathlessly.

"Soon. Very soon. I hope."

"Hey, girls." Beth Raines came up to them and hugged Mandy. "Looking good, Mandy. Listen, your mom is here to pick you up. We'll take care of Butterball for you. And we'll see you in two weeks, okay?"

After the little girl had made her way slowly and clumsily toward her mother, Beth turned to Samantha.

"The Pony Commandos are great, aren't they? I can't believe the progress each of them has shown since we've begun these riding lessons. The exercises that Janet and I were doing with them were helping, but these ponies have really set them free. I think when they're in the saddle, they just have so much more mobility—they can get to where they're going really fast. It's perked up their spirits unbelievably. Especially Mandy. I was starting to worry about her. She has an unflappable spirit, but the frustration and pain of being physically limited was really getting to her. She's truly blossomed in the last few weeks—she's a different kid."

"I'm really glad," Samantha said, touched by Beth's words. "Hey, I guess I'll be seeing a lot more of you in a few days, when Dad gets back."

Beth's pretty face broke into a smile. "I can't wait to see him."

"Me either," Samantha said, returning her smile. She could finally say that she was happy Beth had come into both her and her father's life.

8

THE NEXT WEEK WENT BY IN A BLUR. IAN MCLEAN CAME home with a triumphant Blues King and three other Whitebrook horses who had been getting racing experience down at Gulfstream. Samantha was really glad to have her father home again. At night as she was falling asleep, she could hear him puttering around in the living room, watching TV. In the morning when she got up, he was already pouring himself a cup of coffee. It was very comforting. Now that he, Ashleigh, and Mike were all back at Whitebrook, Samantha's life took on its old rhythm of Shining, school, Tor, and her friends. She no longer felt so stressed about whether all the farm work was getting done properly.

Two days after her father returned, Tor, Samantha, Yvonne, and Gregg all double-dated to the Henry Clay Sadie Hawkins dance. Yvonne came over early, and the two girls got ready at Samantha's house. They had eagerly accepted Beth's offer to do their hair.

Looking in the mirror at her elegant chignon, Samantha's eyes were round. "Wow—I love it. I look so much older, don't I, Yvonne?"

Yvonne nodded, crowding next to Samantha to see her black curls spilling down one side of her head. "We both do. Beth, you're a miracle worker."

Beth smiled. "Both of you have great hair. But I think you know more about French-braiding a horse's mane than dealing with what's on your own heads."

Laughing, Samantha said, "You may be right."

Then the girls had to wait anxiously for Tor and Gregg to pick them up. Gregg had borrowed his mother's new car, since he and Tor both drove pickup trucks.

Tor rang the doorbell, and Samantha breathlessly answered the door. *Wow.* Tor looked fabulous in a dark blue suit, white shirt, and flowered tie. When he looked at Samantha, she was gratified to see his eyes light up.

"You look beautiful," he said slowly, taking in the raspberry-pink, tea-length dress she had picked out so carefully.

Smiling, Samantha said, "Thanks. You do, too. Look great, I mean."

After that it seemed the four of them never stopped smiling. It was crisply cold in the late February night air, but the auditorium was warm with dancing bodies. Samantha had helped to decorate it with colorful streamers and loads of balloons.

Later the band played a slow song, and Tor wordlessly swept Samantha into his arms. They moved together smoothly on the wooden floor, swaying gently back and forth to the music, and Samantha thought she had never felt so happy. Someone dimmed the lights, and Tor gently kissed her hair, then her forehead, then her cheek.

Around midnight Tor walked her to her front door, while Gregg and Yvonne waited in the car.

"I felt so lucky tonight—being there with the most beautiful girl," he said softly, brushing back a loose tendril of her hair. Samantha smiled at him, not even feeling the brisk night breeze. "I'm really glad we're together," she whispered back. "Not just tonight, but all the time."

"Me too." He kissed her again, and then she went inside, the scent of her rose corsage still floating around her hair.

Every day before school Samantha worked Shining on the longe line, always trying to end their lesson on a good note. On Monday morning as she was busy with Shining, the sound of a car's engine interrupted her thoughts. She looked up to see Brad and Lavinia's Ferrari kicking up gravel along the Whitebrook drive.

Groaning to herself, Samantha tried to put all of her attention on Shining. The filly was working well on the longe, and Samantha was determined not to let anything interfere with her training.

As usual, Brad and Lavinia looked perfectly put

together. Samantha figured Lavinia got out of bed every morning with every hair in place. It was sickening.

Without a word of greeting, they paused to watch Samantha. Samantha tried to ignore them. Brushing a strand of hair off her brow, she clicked her tongue, and Shining went smoothly into a well-paced trot. Her reconditioned muscles flowed like oiled rope under her coat, which was starting to take on a healthy silkiness and shine. The carefully thought-out diet that Samantha and Len had been giving her had not only added needed weight but given her a new, sleek appearance. Her mane and tail had grown out some and bounced saucily as she rounded the circle. There was a lightness to her step that reminded Samantha strongly of Wonder. If this filly had one tenth of Wonder's heart, Samantha knew they could have a winner on their hands.

Brad leaned his arms on the top rail and dangled his sunglasses from his fingers. "What do you know," he said to Lavinia. "Mike's finally found a halfway decent filly."

"At least this one's better than the glue-factory candidate we saw the last time we were here. Of course, she's not in the same class as Her Majesty."

Samantha pretended to ignore them, but she heard every word clearly. She smiled secretly to herself. *If Lavinia only knew,* she thought gleefully. *Shining's bloodlines put Her Majesty's to shame!*

She concentrated her thoughts on Shining and signaled her to pick up the pace to a canter. The filly moved smoothly and gracefully into the faster pace.

She really was a joy to watch. Samantha circled her twice, then signaled her to stop.

"Good girl!" she called. "That's the way." Shining had her neck arched as if she knew she'd done an outstanding job. Samantha fished in her pocket and fed the filly a bit of carrot as a reward, then she lovingly rubbed Shining's neck and ears.

Behind her she heard another voice and turned to see that Mike had joined Brad and Lavinia. He was polite, but just barely. Samantha knew he resented the way they came and went so freely on his property, but saying anything to them would only increase the friction Ashleigh already had to put up with.

Samantha listened more carefully as she led Shining out of the ring. Mike motioned to her to join them. Reluctantly she did so, noticing that Brad was examining Shining with real interest.

"You got this filly at that New Jersey sale?" Brad was saying to Mike. "Impossible. I saw the horses you picked up. They were a mess." Brad has never been known for his tact, Samantha thought.

"Shining was definitely one of them, although she looked a little different then," Mike responded.

"Is this that decrepit-looking filly?" Lavinia gasped in disbelief. "It can't be."

"I wasn't there when you saw her," Mike said, "but she probably is."

"It's the same one," Samantha confirmed. Shining gave a playful little prance, and Samantha felt her heart swell with pride at how far the filly had come.

"Well, I suppose she'll make a decent enough

pleasure horse," Lavinia said disparagingly.

Mike smiled. "Oh, you don't know her breeding, then?"

"It can't be much, if she came from that New Jersey stable," Lavinia said with a smirk.

Now it was Samantha's turn to smile as Mike continued mildly, "Actually, she's extremely well-bred. She's one of Townsend Pride's fillies, out of Brite Morn. She's Wonder's half-sister."

Lavinia's pretty mouth had fallen open. Then her cheeks flushed hotly. "I don't believe it. No offspring of Townsend Pride would ever have ended up in the condition she was in."

Brad, still studying Shining, had remained thoughtfully silent during the conversation. Now he turned to Mike. "She was foaled on a Maryland farm?"

Mike nodded.

Brad was scowling. "I remember seeing the mare's name in Townsend Pride's book. In fact, she was bred to him again this year. How old is the filly?"

"Three," Mike replied.

"What are your plans for her?" Brad asked.

Mike glanced over at Samantha. "Well, that's not up to me. Actually, she's Sammy's horse. Sammy's been reconditioning her."

Samantha saw to her delight that Lavinia looked ready to faint.

"Yours?" Lavinia cried, glaring at Samantha.

Smiling cheerfully, Samantha nodded. "That's right. And I think she just might show the same kind of talent as Wonder." Of course, Samantha didn't know that—she wouldn't have any idea of Shining's talent until she started retraining her on the track— but she couldn't resist getting in a dig.

"So you *are* planning to race her," Brad said.

Samantha lifted her shoulders casually. "It's a possibility. I haven't made any firm plans for her. But she *is* doing nicely." *Let them do some guessing and worrying,* she thought.

"Well, is Ashleigh here?" Brad asked, his eyes still narrowed on Shining. "I came over to talk to her."

Wordlessly, Samantha gestured to the mares' barn, where she knew Ashleigh and Mr. Reese were examining Fleet Goddess. The mare had been restless and off her feed since the day before, which could mean that she was about to foal. It killed Samantha that she had to go to school today. She always hated missing the birth of one of the foals.

Twenty minutes later Shining had been cooled out and groomed and was contentedly munching her breakfast back in her stall. Samantha came running out of the McLean cottage, her book bag thrown over a shoulder. At the end of the driveway the dust from Brad and Lavinia's car was just starting to fade. Mike and Ashleigh were standing in the driveway, talking quietly. Samantha glanced at her watch. "Where's Yvonne? We're going to miss the first bell."

"Mike was just telling me about your little encounter with Brad and Lavinia," Ashleigh said with a chuckle.

"They didn't recognize Shining," Samantha said

smugly. "Brad said we'd finally gotten a halfway decent filly."

"That's great!" Ashleigh said wickedly. "You'll show them, Sammy. Actually, Brad was here to talk about breeding Wonder again. Clay Townsend and I had discussed it last week but hadn't made any decisions. Brad's come up with a good idea. He wants to breed her to Midnight Sprinter, and for once I actually agree with him."

Frowning, Samantha thought for a moment. "I remember him. He came in second in the Derby one year, didn't he? He's the big bay over at Townsend Acres."

"Yep. He's a good horse. We'll breed her in early April, if the vet says it's okay."

"That sounds great," Samantha said. "Oh, there's Yvonne! I have to run!"

Early on Thursday morning, Samantha dropped a kiss on Shining's nose. "Good-bye, girl," she said softly, rubbing between Shining's ears. Samantha was leaving in a minute to go to the National Horse Show with Yvonne, Tor, and Gregg. "Ashleigh is going to take care of you while I'm gone, and she said she'd work you, too. You'll be fine, but I'll miss you." Quickly she dropped another kiss on the filly's soft nose. Shining whickered in response. On Samantha's way out, she couldn't resist peeking over the stall wall at Fleet Goddess and her new foal, a colt they had named Fleeting Moment.

"Hey, Goddess. How's your baby?" Samantha

said. The foal was only two days old, but already he was stepping around the stall with confidence and nursing vigorously. He was a solid jet black, except for a very small white star on his forehead. Right now he was still curled up on the clean straw on the floor, fast asleep like a little fawn. Fleet Goddess looked down at him proudly.

"He's beautiful, girl. Good job."

Goddess huffed her agreement, and then Samantha went out into the chilly morning air in time to see Mr. Nelson, Tor's father, pull up in their truck, towing a two-horse van.

They were exhausted by the time they arrived at the show arena and settled Cisco, but the next morning Samantha, Tor, and Gregg watched as Yvonne led Cisco through some practice moves in a small ring set up for that purpose. The next day would be the actual show, and the huge ring would be cleared, then jumps would be set up for all the different competitions. Cisco had made the trip well and seemed relaxed and confident as he went through his familiar exercises.

When Yvonne rode Cisco out of the ring, she looked marginally calmer than she had earlier that morning.

"You looked great, Yvonne," Gregg told her, taking Cisco's bridle so she could dismount. "You just have to keep telling yourself how good you are—if you weren't, you and Cisco never would have made it this far. Remember what it said in the NHS program?

In your division, you and your competitors are the top sixteen riders your age."

Yvonne smiled at him. "Thanks, Gregg. And thanks to you two," she said to Tor and Samantha. "It means a lot to me to have you all here, supporting me. I just hope I don't let you down."

"Then you're ready to go out on the town tonight?" Tor asked teasingly.

"Yeah—I am," Yvonne answered.

"Even though I've been here before, New York always seems overwhelming," Samantha said a couple of hours later, tucking her arm through Tor's. After seeing Cisco safely stabled at the Meadowlands in New Jersey, they had left Mr. Nelson to watch him and crossed the Hudson River into Manhattan. Now they were walking down Fifth Avenue, bemusedly taking in all the impressive specialty shops and designer boutiques. It was cold, colder than it had been in Kentucky, and a strong wind was whipping down the tunnel created by the walls of the skyscrapers.

Behind them, Yvonne seemed preoccupied and worried, though Gregg was trying to take her mind off things. After a while the excitement of New York seemed to be doing the trick.

The next morning dawned clear and cold at the Meadowlands in northern New Jersey. Samantha was up early to help Yvonne get ready. The novice competition was the very first one that morning, so Yvonne changed into her riding habit at their hotel. Then they rounded up Gregg and Tor and headed to the large sports complex a short distance from the hotel.

Once there, Gregg and Tor went to check out some of the advertisers' exhibits on the lower level of the arena, promising to be back within half an hour. The two girls headed immediately to the temporary canvas stalls set up in back of the complex. Since the Meadowlands wasn't designed solely for equestrian events, no permanent stabling was available.

They found Mr. Nelson reading the paper and drinking coffee from a Styrofoam cup outside Cisco's stall.

"He slept well, no problems," Mr. Nelson reported, and Samantha and Yvonne set to work making Cisco look his best.

As usual Cisco seemed to pick up on the feeling of excitement in the air, and snorted impatiently at the two girls, as though to say, "Let's get going—I want to show everyone my stuff."

Yvonne managed a wobbly grin at Samantha. "Two hours from now, it will all be over—for me, anyway."

Each day of the five-day show was packed from early morning to late evening with competitions, exhibitions, warm-ups, and award ceremonies. In a way Samantha was glad that Yvonne was competing on the second day of the show—that meant she didn't have extra time to get even more nervous. And afterward they could enjoy watching the many hunter competitions, as well as pony shows, equitation programs, and training awards.

The night before in their hotel room, too excited to

sleep, Samantha and Yvonne had pored over every page of their programs. Samantha had squealed with excitement when they found Yvonne's name on the list of riders in the novice division. In the other competitor lists, they had recognized names of riders who had dominated their sport for years, including one eighteen-year-old boy who had been judged best junior jumper for the last three years.

"I'm glad I'm not going against him," Yvonne had said with relief.

Now, as they finished Cisco's grooming in his temporary stall, Yvonne still looked as though she was feeling some fear. But when she looked into Cisco's intelligent brown eyes, a new glint of determination crossed her face. "You deserve this, boy," she told him. "I'm going to do my best by you. Now let's go get 'em!"

"You'll be fine, you know," Samantha said quietly.

She was going to continue, but then Tor tapped on the stall door and said, "Yvonne? Time to walk the course."

This was the first opportunity any of the riders would have to see the course before they jumped it. As soon as Yvonne had walked the jumping course with the other riders, she would take Cisco to wait for their turn, and Samantha would join Mr. Nelson, Tor, and Gregg up in the stands to watch Yvonne ride.

When Yvonne came back from walking the course, she was visibly trembling. Her black eyes looked panicked. Her earlier determination seemed to have faded away.

"Sam," she whispered hoarsely, "the course is much more difficult than anything I've ever jumped."

"Just relax," Samantha said pleadingly to her friend. "Quit panicking. You won't be riding until eighth. You'll be able to watch the other riders for trouble spots."

Gripping Samantha's arm fiercely, Yvonne suddenly burst out, "I can't do it, Sammy. I just can't. Please, let's just go home."

Cisco, reacting to the emotional exchange, pulled on his bridle, his eyes rolling. Samantha made soothing sounds and patted his nose.

"Listen, Yvonne," Tor broke in firmly, a frown on his handsome face, "I thought we'd been through all this before! The show committee has judged you one of the top juvenile riders in the country. You have the experience, ranking, and points to make it this far. If you allow fear to sabotage your performance now, you'll be insulting the committee, the other riders, and even Cisco. Not to mention me, your teacher, because I think you're ready to do this. Now, you have to decide what you're going to do, and what you've been training for this past year. And until you do, stay away from Cisco, because you're upsetting him." Still frowning, Tor strode away, looking almost angry.

Surprised, Samantha stared after him. She had never seen Tor like that, but then he was a top show jumper himself and felt very deeply about the sport. She turned back to Yvonne, ready to soften his words somehow, but Yvonne's expression had calmed, and she looked subdued.

"He's right. I deserved that—I'm being stupid. I don't know what's wrong with me. Come on, Cisco, let's go warm up," she said resolutely, facing her horse. "We'll be up soon." Swinging expertly into the saddle, Yvonne looked down to smile unsteadily at Samantha. "I'm going to walk him a bit—go up to the stands and root for me."

"You got it," Samantha promised.

The course was indeed difficult, Samantha saw. There were combination jumps, two water jumps, and numerous switchbacks and tight turns. Samantha knew Yvonne had walked it earlier, mentally counting strides between the fences, determining the best angle for approach, how tight a turn would shave precious seconds off their score and yet keep Cisco at the proper rhythm and pace for the next jump. Samantha had watched Tor do the same thing at quite a few competitions.

The first three riders had gone while Samantha and Tor were with Yvonne, but now they watched tensely as the next four riders went, one after the other. No one had gone clean yet, and one horse had stumbled badly, spilling his rider into a water jump. Samantha understood how bitterly disappointed the rider, a sixteen-year-old boy from Connecticut, must feel.

Then it was Yvonne's turn. Nervously Samantha sucked down her soda, her eyes glued on Yvonne's elegant figure in her tight-fitting fawn breeches, riding coat, black velvet hard hat, and shiny black knee-high boots. Cisco pranced eagerly into the ring.

Yvonne looked in the direction of the judges' stand and saluted the panel.

Samantha heard Gregg whisper hoarsely, "She looks great. I just hope she can hold her nerves together."

Silently Samantha nodded.

Then Yvonne put Cisco into a smooth, collected canter as they circled around to the first jump. Sitting forward eagerly in her seat, Samantha gripped Tor's hand so tightly her knuckles were white. With a grimace Tor shook his hand free, then kissed her cheek and put his arm around her shoulders.

"Come on, Yvonne, you can do it," Samantha said under her breath.

Most evidence of Yvonne's nervousness was gone as she sat tall and straight in the small, light jumping saddle. Samantha knew she had memorized as much of the course as possible and had already worked out some kind of strategy. The first jump was a high gate, and Yvonne collected Cisco's pace, aimed him, then squeezed her legs against his sides at exactly the right moment. They went over beautifully, with room to spare, and Samantha saw Yvonne's face relax a little.

Next was a combination jump, two fences put close together so that Yvonne had to squeeze, jump, take one short stride, then squeeze and jump again. Again they went over effortlessly, Yvonne keeping Cisco's pace collected for the second jump, then giving him rein and leaning her body with him with an instinct born of long hours of practice.

As Samantha, Tor, and Gregg watched, Yvonne cleared the first water jump, then a high brush jump, then a wall, followed closely by a double oxer.

To Samantha, the time it took Yvonne to finish her circuit seemed both much too short and also somehow endless. At the end Yvonne had only two faults, and her timing was well within the acceptable range. As soon as she had cleared the last fence and headed Cisco out of the ring, Samantha, Tor, and Gregg all jumped up and began cheering.

They waited to see her final results and saw Yvonne and Cisco called into the ring as ribbon finishers.

"Way to go, Yvonne!" Samantha yelled, already scrambling down out of the stands to go meet her friend.

"I don't know why I was so nervous," Yvonne bubbled, carefully attaching her white fourth-place ribbon to her blazer.

Cisco whinnied.

"You did great, Yvonne," Gregg said, hugging her proudly. "You're the fourth-best novice jumper in the country!"

"Cisco was amazing," Yvonne said modestly. "He knew what to do without my even telling him."

"Well, in honor of your terrific performance, when we head home, Sammy and I will ride in the van with Cisco, and you and Gregg can ride up front with Dad," Tor offered.

Gregg accepted without hesitation. "I thank you, and my behind thanks you."

"And I thank you, too, Tor," Yvonne said shyly, stepping up to him. "If you hadn't given me that pep talk before the show and really woken me up, I don't know what would have happened."

"At the time I thought I was too rough on you. But now I think I should have cracked a whip over your head—then you'd have gotten first place," Tor said with a laugh.

Yvonne chuckled and hugged him quickly. "No thanks. A tough speech was plenty!"

The ride back to Kentucky was rather chilly and uncomfortable for Samantha and Tor, sitting tightly together on a bale of hay in the empty half of the horse van, but they didn't notice it that much.

"You're a good teacher, Tor Nelson," Samantha said dreamily after they had pulled back from a long kiss.

"At kissing or jumping?" Tor teased huskily.

Samantha laughed. "Both."

9

EARLY MONDAY MORNING SAMANTHA WAS WORKING Shining on the longe when Ashleigh came to watch at the small training oval.

"How did she do while I was gone?" Samantha called. They had gotten back so late the night before, she hadn't had a chance to talk to Ashleigh.

Ashleigh shook her head ruefully. "She was fine, but she didn't work as well for me as for you. I think she might be a one-woman horse, just like Wonder was. Right now, for you, she looks beautiful."

Indeed, Shining was moving effortlessly through her paces, changing from one gait to another without hesitation as Samantha asked her.

"Oh, Mandy called yesterday afternoon. I told her how Yvonne did, and she was really excited," Ashleigh said.

"I'm supposed to see her this afternoon after school." Samantha signaled Shining to slow to a

111

walk. "She was so disappointed that we had to cancel yesterday's Pony Commando lesson because we were all gone," Samantha continued. "And I know she missed hearing about Shining. But I'll bring her over here today, and she can help me groom this pretty girl, right, Shining?"

As Ashleigh and Samantha watched, Shining gave a small whinny and shook her elegant head.

At school Samantha found Yvonne bubbling again, this time to Maureen O'Brien and Stacy Halpern.

"Wow—no wonder you were nervous," Stacy said. "A cousin of mine wanted to enter the National Horse Show, and I remember how tense he was, waiting for that letter of acceptance. He didn't get in. Each year they turn away hundreds of people, you know."

Yvonne groaned. "Don't remind me. Even though it's all over, I'll get nervous again."

They laughed, then Maureen said, "Can you write an article about the horse show for the *Herald,* Sam? I know a lot of kids are really interested in it."

Samantha agreed right away. "I'd love to. I even took notes while I was there, in case you wanted me to put together something. Hey, did anyone hear back from their colleges yet?"

Stacy shook her head. "I'm taking a year off to help my mom with her hardware store. I'll apply to college next year."

Maureen nodded. "I heard. I can't believe I almost forgot to tell you guys. I got accepted into Northwestern's journalism program early in January."

"That's terrific! You're so lucky to have heard already," Samantha said.

"Yeah, but we should be hearing any day now, too, Sammy," Yvonne said. She and Samantha had both applied to the University of Kentucky at Lexington.

"The waiting is making me crazy," Samantha complained. "Especially since it's the only place I applied to."

"Well, you can take your mind off it for one night and come to the basketball game with us after school. Call Tor and have him meet us," Maureen suggested.

"That sounds great," Samantha said, "but this afternoon Mandy Jarvis is coming over. I can't disappoint her. Count me in for the next game."

"Will do," Maureen promised.

"It felt like you were gone longer than four days," Mandy said that afternoon as she carefully brushed Shining's legs.

Samantha was concentrating on removing a tangle from the filly's mane, which was growing in nicely, but she turned to smile down at the little girl. "I missed you, too," she said. "And so did Shining."

"You know what?" Mandy stopped brushing. "I asked Mama and Daddy for a horse of my own. For my birthday. It's next month, in April."

"Oh, that would be wonderful, Mandy. What did they say?"

Mandy shrugged. "They said they would see." Then an impish smile crossed her face. "That usually means yes."

Samantha laughed. "You tell your mom and dad that if they need advice about where to get a horse, they can talk to me, or my dad, or Tor. Okay?"

"Okay," Mandy agreed happily.

After thoroughly grooming Shining, Samantha took Mandy to see Flurry and Midnight, who were getting bigger and bolder every day. Flurry was becoming Shining's special friend, in the same way that Sidney, one of the other barn cats, seemed to be Wonder's Pride's favorite buddy. Flurry was always risking the high climb up Shining's stall door in order to wash herself importantly under the filly's patient gaze.

Later Mandy exclaimed over Fleeting Moment, Fleet Goddess's little colt.

"Such a little baby horse!" she cried, clapping her small hands.

Fleeting Moment, who had absolutely no fear of strangers despite his age and small size, nosed his way over to the chain crossing the stall door.

Gently Mandy patted his tiny black nose.

"Can I give him a treat?" she asked.

"He's too little yet," Samantha explained. "He's still drinking only his mother's milk."

Mandy looked shyly at Samantha. "Maybe my parents could buy me this horse for my birthday."

Samantha thought for a moment. "I'm not sure," she said honestly. "If he has real potential as a racer, Mike will want to keep him and train him to race. If he looks like he doesn't have much potential, I'm not sure how expensive he would be. And at any rate, he'll need to stay with his mother for almost another six months. So I guess we'll just have to wait and see, but your parents should probably consider other horses." Samantha knew Mandy's parents were well off, but she wasn't sure if they would indulge Mandy's desire for a horse, with a Thoroughbred.

Mandy nodded. "Okay."

"Besides, you want a horse you can ride right away, don't you?" Samantha asked practically. "Fleeting Moment won't be ready to ride for almost two years."

"Oh, no—I need to ride one as soon as I get it," Mandy agreed seriously.

A few days later, Samantha decided Shining was ready to be ridden under tack. It was the second week of March, and the famous Kentucky bluegrass was beginning to turn green in the pastures surrounding Whitebrook. The days were longer and mild, though the nights frequently were still chilly. In the two months since Shining had been at Whitebrook, she had undergone a transformation. Powerful muscles rippled under her silky coat. Her mane was long and flowing, and there was a definite spring in her step.

"And she eats like a—well, like a horse," Len said cheerfully.

Samantha put Shining into the crossties in the middle of the center aisle. She was unsure how Shining would react to the saddle, since she hadn't been ridden in months, but the filly stood patiently as Samantha tacked her up.

115

Then, while Ashleigh and Len watched, Samantha led the filly to the stable yard. Ashleigh held Shining's bridle so Samantha could mount, and for the first time Shining seemed to understand what was about to happen.

Just as Samantha was putting her boot in the stirrup, Shining danced sideways. Samantha had to hop after her with one foot in a stirrup. The filly's eyes were wide, and she turned back to look at Samantha uneasily.

"Shh," Samantha soothed her. "It's okay, girl. It's just me—no one else. You're doing so well, and I think you're ready for a rider. But it will be only me, and no one but me. Okay? Want to give it a try?"

At Samantha's voice, Shining blew out her breath, but seemed to quiet a little. Holding her own breath, Samantha slowly and carefully pulled herself up into the light saddle and gathered the reins in her hands. She took a handful of Shining's mane in her hands, too, just to be on the safe side in case Shining decided to buck.

Shining danced a little to the side again, and again she craned her neck around to eye Samantha in her saddle.

"Good girl," Samantha praised her, barely able to believe that she was finally in the saddle of her very own horse. "That's a girl. We're not going to do anything fancy, okay? Why don't we just take a little walk around the barn?"

Gently Samantha reined Shining around the stable yard, with Ashleigh and Len watching. She could feel the tension in Shining's muscles—Shining definitely wasn't entirely happy having a rider on her back again. Samantha could only conclude that some rider had badly mishandled her in the past, using pain instead of reward to get the filly to do what they wanted.

Gradually, though, as Samantha spoke soothingly to her, Shining began to relax. Samantha was careful to make no quick or startling moves. If she could just get Shining up and down the lane by the mares' barn today, she would be happy.

She turned Shining in the direction of the lane. "You've been out here with me before," she told the filly. "There's nothing to be nervous about."

Shining snorted, but the farther they walked, the more Samantha could feel her relaxing, accepting the presence of a rider again. She really seemed to trust Samantha.

When they reached the end of the lane, Samantha felt confident enough to trot Shining back. As she tightened her legs on Shining's flanks, she waited for a sign of hesitation. But there was none. Shining switched gaits obediently and trotted with a springing step over the grass. Samantha smiled with relief and joy. "Good girl!"

She still couldn't get over the fact that she was riding her very own Thoroughbred. It was like a dream come true. And the fact that Shining was half-sister to one of Samantha's favorite horses, and that Samantha herself had helped perform a turnaround in Shining's health, sweetened the reality until Samantha felt as though she would simply burst with happiness.

Still, Samantha knew this ride was only a small step forward in Shining's training. The horse could now be ridden over Whitebrook's trails, which would help to further condition her, but in no way did this one ride guarantee her future as a racer. After Shining got used to being ridden on the trails, Samantha would start riding her in the training oval. But since Shining had probably had bad experiences connected with her training, Samantha would have to proceed carefully.

As she approached the stable yard, she saw that Ashleigh and Len were still waiting for her, eager to hear her evaluation of the filly's potential.

Obediently Shining slowed to a walk, then stopped. Ashleigh held her bridle while Samantha dismounted.

"One down," Samantha said happily. "She was really nervous when we started out, but she's relaxed now. Aren't you, girl?" Samantha kissed Shining's silky neck.

"She looked good, from what I could see," Ashleigh said with a grin. "You've really done an amazing job in reconditioning her."

"Thanks!" Samantha started to lead Shining back to the barn, but looked up when she heard the sound of a car coming up the long gravel driveway.

Samantha recognized Clay Townsend's car. Now in his late fifties, Clay Townsend was considered one of the foremost breeders and trainers in Kentucky, if not in America. With his short-cropped gray hair, tanned face, and athletic figure, he looked every inch the traditional horseman.

Smiling, he got out of his car and came to greet them. Shaking Mike's hand, he said, "Congratulations on Blues King's win down at Gulfstream. He's a nice horse. And you just got back from your honeymoon, right?"

Mike nodded.

Then Mr. Townsend said, "I hear you have one of Townsend Pride's fillies. Brad was telling me about her—said you'd found her at an auction. I'd love to take a look at her."

Although she tried to keep a neutral expression on her face, Samantha couldn't help frowning inside at the thought that Brad and Lavinia might start meddling and interfering again.

"Here she is," Ashleigh said, motioning to Shining. "But she's Sammy's filly, not mine," Ashleigh continued. "When Mike found her, she was in pretty bad shape, but Sammy's bringing her back."

Samantha held Shining's bridle as Mr. Townsend looked the filly over. "I can see some of her sire," he said thoughtfully, rubbing his chin. "She's a good-looking horse."

"Now she is," Ashleigh responded with a smile. "You should have seen her when she arrived."

"Brad says you may race her. Is that so?"

Ashleigh shrugged. "Maybe, but that's up to Sammy."

"Right, right." Mr. Townsend gave Samantha a smile. "Well, Brad and I would be very interested to hear how she's coming along."

Nodding tightly, Samantha led Shining back into the barn so she could be rubbed down, groomed, and fed. The elder Townsend's interest in Shining made her uneasy—she didn't trust anyone in that family, though she knew Ashleigh usually had a pretty good working relationship with Mr. Townsend.

10

AS THE MARCH DAYS GREW WARMER, THE PACE PICKED UP rapidly at Whitebrook. Samantha and Tor concentrated on preparing Sierra for the 'chase in early April, working him over the hurdles on the turf course several times a week. Samantha took Shining for longer and longer jogs over the trails, conditioning her muscles, building her stamina. Although she had her fears about how Shining would react to going on the track again, she worked toward that goal and hoped to have the filly ready soon.

It was the happiest spring of Samantha's life. Always her favorite season of the year, the renewed sunlight seemed to give her extra energy, so that she fairly flew through her chores, her schoolwork, the housework she shared with her father. And this year, the first year in which she was training her very own Thoroughbred, was especially satisfying.

Early one Saturday in the middle of March, Tor

came to Whitebrook to work Sierra. Now that the ground wasn't frozen anymore, the big liver-chestnut could be worked on Whitebrook's turf course.

After a great workout over the hedgelike fences they had set up around the oval, Tor dismounted and led Sierra over to where Samantha was sitting on the fence.

"He's doing great," Tor said. "Like he'd never missed a practice. Let's talk to Mike about entering him in the Aiken 'chase. And after that, who knows? There are a couple of important 'chases up in New England that we could aim him at, later this spring."

Affectionately Tor patted the big horse's neck. Sierra dipped his head and started sniffing around for possible hidden carrots.

"Okay, okay," Samantha said, laughing. "You've made your point." She pulled a carrot out of her windbreaker pocket and broke it into chunks, feeding it to Sierra a piece at a time. He lipped them up quickly, as if to show Samantha he knew he deserved them.

Tor shook his head. "Does the word 'spoiled' mean anything to you?"

Samantha was still laughing when her father walked toward the stable yard, waving a white envelope.

"Sammy! Mail's here. Something for you."

Frowning, Samantha looked at the return address on the envelope. "It's from the U of K at Lexington." She turned worried green eyes to her father and Tor. "What if I didn't get in?"

Mr. McLean put a hand on her shoulder. "Open the envelope, honey."

Holding her breath, she carefully pushed her thumbnail under the envelope flap, ripping it open. While her father and Tor waited silently, she unfolded the letter and read the printed words.

Dear Ms. McLean,

We're pleased to inform you of your acceptance into the undergraduate program at the University of Kentucky at Lexington. This letter will be followed by an admissions packet detailing the courses and fees . . .

A slow smile spread over Samantha's face, then she threw her arms around her father and squeezed him tight, before turning to receive an embrace from Tor.

"I made it! Just like Ashleigh! They accepted me!"

Samantha immediately called Yvonne, who had just received her letter of acceptance, too.

"So are you thinking about living in a dorm, Sam?" Yvonne asked.

"Can't. I wouldn't have as much time with Shining, or any of the other horses. How about you?"

"I might," Yvonne said. "Gregg lives on campus, and it would be fun to be able to spend so much time together. Hey, when's Pride coming home?" she asked, changing the subject. Everyone knew the famous horse was just about fully recovered and ready to return to Whitebrook.

"Tuesday. I'm so thrilled. The farm hasn't been the same without him. On Monday I'm coming right home to make sure his stall is totally ready. I still can't get used to the idea that he'll never race again, but he'll make a great stallion. The most important thing is that he's alive and well and coming home."

"Maybe next week I can come over to see him," Yvonne suggested.

"Name your day."

Shining's training had progressed to the point where Samantha was now giving her two workouts a day—a brief jog every morning and a long work along the trails every afternoon, trotting and galloping. The filly was amazing Samantha with the speed of her improvement and her desire to do well. Shining seemed to revel in each workout.

"I just can't believe she lost every race she was in last summer," Samantha said to Ashleigh when they returned from their work on Sunday. "I can feel this spark in her—like she really would love to get out there and compete."

"Just remember the kind of training she must have received—you had to take her back to the beginning. And she certainly wasn't being well treated, either. I'm not a bit surprised she didn't run well, even if those races were at the bottom of the heap. Maybe it's time you took her out on the oval," Ashleigh suggested.

"That's exactly what I was thinking. I'm a little concerned about how she's going to react," Samantha said. "The track can't bring back good memories for her, but if she's ever going to race again, she needs to overcome her fears and start working on the oval."

"It might be a good idea to work her with a pace horse the first few times," Ashleigh said thoughtfully. "Having another horse nearby might help keep her calm. I'd be glad to take one of the exercise ponies out with you."

"Would you?" Samantha said. "That would be great, Ash!"

"How about tomorrow afternoon after school?" Ashleigh asked. "It's too hectic in the mornings with all the other horses on the track."

"That sounds perfect. Mandy's coming over tomorrow afternoon. I know she'll get a thrill out of watching Shining's first trip around the oval."

On Monday afternoon Samantha couldn't believe how nervous she felt about taking Shining out on the oval. By the time Mandy's parents dropped her off, Samantha's hands were clammy from nerves, and her stomach was busy flip-flopping. She tried to tell herself that if it didn't go well today, there would be other days. But it was becoming increasingly important to her that Shining go back to the races.

Samantha already had Shining and one of the exercise ponies tacked up, and Ashleigh held them as Samantha went to greet Mandy and help her up onto the stool she always used to watch the workouts.

Mandy's eyes had widened with excitement when she saw Shining. "Are you going to ride her today?" she asked breathlessly.

"You're going to see a special event today. I'm going to take her out on the track for the first time."

Mandy clapped. "All right! What's the matter? You look scared."

Samantha gave the little girl a sheepish grin. "Well, I am, a little—but I'll get over it. We'll try and do a good job—just for you."

With Mandy settled and Len standing protectively beside the girl, Samantha rejoined Ashleigh. Moments later they were in the saddle and heading through the gap onto the oval. It was a beautiful March afternoon and the sun was warm on Samantha's back, but at the moment she was too intent on the ride ahead to notice it much.

Immediately Samantha knew that Shining was uneasy. She flicked her elegant ears back and forth as she stepped onto the harrowed dirt of the oval. Her delicate nostrils widened, and she snorted unhappily. Samantha could feel the tension running through the filly's body like an electric current. Samantha mentally braced herself. This wasn't going to be an easy trip.

She glanced over at Ashleigh. Ashleigh had noticed Shining's state. "We'll just take it slow and easy," Ashleigh said softly. "Start walking them up the track."

Samantha nodded and gently urged Shining forward. At first the filly refused to move. She eyed her surroundings and snorted again. "It's all right," Samantha soothed. She urged Shining forward again with pressure from her seat in the saddle. Shining took several hesitant steps. They drew abreast of Ashleigh. Side by side they continued at a walk up the track.

Suddenly Shining snorted loudly. Her legs danced beneath her and she skittered sideways across the track, bumping Ashleigh and her mount. Samantha tightened her right rein and got the filly under control, all the while talking to her, reassuring her.

Shining didn't seem to be listening, though. She was too caught up in old, bad memories. Suddenly she gathered her muscles and took off like a shot up the track. Samantha had been prepared for anything, so she was ready for the filly's bolt. Her grip on the reins was firm. She sank her heels deeper in the stirrup irons. "Okay, have it your way," she said softly to Shining. "Go ahead, get it out of your system, run your fears out."

And Shining was definitely running from sights and scenes Samantha could only imagine. Her galloping strides ate up the distance as they pounded around the first turn. Samantha heard hoofbeats behind her and knew Ashleigh was coming in pursuit, but Samantha still had control of the filly. Shining hadn't taken the bit in her teeth.

"Just run it out . . . run it out," Samantha repeated. Her greatest fear was that the mad gallop would take too much out of Shining, but she didn't think she'd have any success in trying to pull her up now, either. From their works on the trails, Shining had regained a lot of muscle tone and condition, but she wasn't ready for a long, breakneck gallop. Samantha knew the filly would be lathered in sweat when she finally stopped.

From the corner of her eye Samantha saw Ashleigh

just behind and outside them. Her exercise pony was game, but he couldn't gain any more ground on Shining. *Well, she has speed,* Samantha thought, wondering if she'd run as fast when she wasn't frightened out of her mind.

Gradually, as they rounded the far turn of the mile oval, Shining began to respond to the pressure Samantha was putting on the reins. Her pace became less furious. Her ears flicked back when Samantha called to her. "Easy, girl, easy. Let's slow it down. There's nothing to be afraid of."

Halfway through the turn, Shining dropped into a slower gallop. Breathing a huge sigh of relief, Samantha stood high in the stirrups and eased the filly back into a canter. She felt the shudder that went through Shining's body. By the time she'd slowed Shining to a trot and Ashleigh drew up beside them, Shining's sides were heaving, and her coat was white with sweat.

"Are you okay?" Ashleigh asked anxiously.

Samantha managed a nod. Her concentration was still totally on Shining.

"I think she's worked it out of her system," Ashleigh said quietly. "Let's try and trot them through another circuit and see if we can calm her down more."

They continued around the track at a trot, Samantha's every sense alert and tuned into Shining. The filly wasn't blowing as hard, and by the time they'd nearly circled the track for a second time, she could feel Shining beginning to relax.

"Okay, girl," Samantha said gently. "I know you were frightened, but it'll be all right now. Just calm down."

Ashleigh was right beside them as they rode off the oval.

Len and Mandy were both staring wide-eyed.

"Whew!" Len said.

"She runs so fast!" Mandy cried. The little girl didn't know that their gallop was unplanned, and Samantha wasn't about to tell her. Len understood, though. He quickly stepped over to hold the bridle and coo softly to Shining when Samantha and the filly came to a stop.

He looked up at Samantha and mouthed the words, "You all right?"

Samantha gave a quick nod, but discovered her knees were shaking when she dismounted and stood beside Shining. Her first thought was Shining's condition, though. Len was already kneeling and running his weathered hands over the filly's legs. "Seems okay," he said with relief.

Samantha let out a long breath.

Len took Shining's reins. "Let me take her and get her sponged down and cooled out."

Before he did, though, Shining turned her head toward Mandy.

As tired as she was, Shining whickered a soft greeting to the girl. Samantha led the filly a step closer.

"That was totally excellent," Mandy said enthusiastically. "You are going to be absolutely the best racehorse!" She took Shining's muzzle in her hands and gently kissed her nose. "I love you, Shining!" she whispered.

Tor picked Samantha up from school the next afternoon. She had told him all about the previous day's adventure on the training oval. "How was Shining this morning?" he asked her with concern.

"She seemed all right, thank heavens," Samantha said. "Len hosed her down and we both cooled her out. She was still a little strung out when I put her in her stall last night, but by this morning she was herself."

"Are you going to give her a few days off before you take her out again?" Tor asked.

Samantha nodded. "At least a day. I'll have plenty to keep me busy this afternoon with Pride coming home!"

"Excited?"

Samantha laughed. "Are you kidding? I can hardly sit still."

"I noticed," Tor said, giving her a wink.

Tor had barely pulled the pickup truck to a halt before Samantha leaped out, dumped her backpack at the edge of her cottage's walk, and ran to the stallion barn. Inside, Ashleigh, Mike, and Mr. McLean were all gathered around the roomy box stall with its brass plaque that read WONDER'S PRIDE.

Ashleigh turned a smiling face to Samantha, and Samantha gasped, "Is he here?"

Laughing, Ashleigh said, "Oh, he's here, all right!"

Everyone moved aside so Samantha could get to

130

Pride's stall. He was contentedly eating from his hay net. At the sight of the handsome Thoroughbred, standing strong and healthy in his stall, tears of happiness sprang to Samantha's eyes. Just a few months ago, everyone had been sure he wouldn't make it. But now here he was again, looking fit and happy, just like his old self.

At the sound of Samantha's voice, Pride turned and eagerly came forward to push his head over the top of the stall door. Samantha threw her arms around his neck and kissed him.

"Oh, Pride! It's so good to have you back. I missed you, boy."

Gently he lipped her red hair, as though to say he felt the same.

For long moments Samantha held him, resting her head against his strong neck, her eyes closed. Then she pulled back and looked at his beloved face all over again.

Turning to Ashleigh, she said, "This is great!"

Ashleigh nodded. "He looks glad to be home. As much as I'm going to miss the excitement of his racing, he can relax and romp in the paddock, and have a few girlfriends," she added with a chuckle. "Mr. Townsend has already talked to me about trying to breed him at the end of the month—we've set pretty high stud fees, but there are plenty of interested breeders."

Samantha continued stroking Pride. "You're back where you belong, big guy," she said happily. "We'll take extra-good care of you now."

Pride whuffed contentedly and gently rested his muzzle on her shoulder.

Samantha took Shining back on the oval the following day. Ashleigh rode out on one of the exercise horses. Although Shining seemed slightly skittish as they entered the oval, she didn't bolt this time. After her first work, when no one hit her or abused her, she seemed to be realizing that the training track didn't necessarily mean pain. Samantha jogged her cautiously, but there weren't any more surprises. She rode off the oval feeling more optimistic.

After a week of gradually stepped-up workouts, Samantha was feeling better and better about Shining's chances. The filly now went out onto the training oval with only the slightest hesitation and soon settled down to business, following Samantha's commands. Shining was going two miles at a slow gallop now, effortlessly. She was listening and responding willingly. She was putting her heart into each work, and Samantha hoped that with each passing day, the filly was also putting her bad memories further behind.

Samantha hadn't breezed Shining yet—she wanted to give the filly plenty of time to relax on the oval without any pressure—but she knew it would soon be time to take the next step.

"She's really looking good," Ashleigh said as Samantha rode off the oval.

Samantha beamed and unfastened her helmet strap.

"I know you and Tor will be busy getting Sierra ready for his 'chase, but do you think you'd like to try breezing her in a couple of days?"

"You bet I would," Samantha said as she dismounted. "I really need to know if her past running style was just bad training. I keep wondering whether she'll kick in when I ask her, and with enough speed to win a race."

"I know she never had the inclination to take the lead in her past races," Ashleigh said, "but I think that had a lot to do with the way she was treated. She wasn't putting her heart into winning. Believe me, the day that she bolted, there was no way I was going to catch her!"

"That wasn't exactly a normal work," Samantha said with a smile as she pulled up the stirrups. Shining seemed to sense they were talking about her. She looked back and forth between the two young women.

"True, but she has speed when she wants to. One important thing you'll have to do is figure out her best running style. She ran midpack in the past," Ashleigh said.

"And never got up better than fourth."

"But she's a different horse now." Ashleigh rubbed Shining's nose. "Aren't you, girl? Time will tell." Ashleigh looked over at Samantha and shook her head in disbelief. "I really can't believe what you've done with her in just three months. Mike and I definitely made the right decision when we gave her to you."

*　　*　　*

That afternoon, Samantha helped Tor give Sierra one of his training sessions before his steeplechase in Aiken. They had set up identical three-and-a-half-foot jumps in a pattern inside the turf course at Whitebrook. After Tor mounted and started Sierra on the course, Samantha waited at the gate with a stop-watch in her hand.

Moving as one, horse and rider cleared the jumps effortlessly, then pounded toward the line Samantha had drawn in the dirt.

As they roared past, Samantha clicked the stop-watch. "Excellent time!" she called as Tor turned Sierra and slowed him to a trot. After Tor had cooled Sierra out sufficiently, Samantha held Sierra's bridle while he dismounted, then handed him an icy can of soda. He gulped it eagerly.

Just then Mike came up.

"How's he doing?"

"Really well."

"Extremely well," Tor echoed.

Mike grinned. "I'm glad he's good at something, 'cause he sure stank as a flat racer. It's thanks to you two that he found his calling."

11

"HOW DO YOU THINK YOU DID ON THAT POP QUIZ?" Yvonne asked Samantha as they walked out of their English class after school on Thursday.

"Ah-choo!" Samantha sneezed, then dug in her backpack for a tissue.

"I'll take that as a yes," Yvonne said with a grin. "It was pretty easy. Hey, just think, two more days, and then you and Tor will go to Sierra's 'chase!'"

"I can't wait," Samantha said. "I'm sure they'll do well. They really make a special team."

"Yeah. Oh, hey, listen—I wanted to ask you. I know you're busy this weekend with the steeplechase and everything. But let's pick a day next week after school to go shopping in Lexington." She grinned wickedly at Samantha's less than enthusiastic expression. "Your favorite activity. But seriously, I need some new summer clothes. I think I actually grew about an inch over the winter," Yvonne moaned. "At this rate, I'm going to end up gargantuan. Poor Cisco's back will be bending under my weight. Good thing I don't have plans to become a jockey."

Samantha let out a laugh, looking skeptically at her friend's tall but extremely willowy figure. "That's the stupidest thing I've ever heard in my life," she said firmly. "Anyway, you should be glad—I haven't grown since I was fifteen. But I guess I can force myself to go shopping with you. How about Tuesday?"

"Perfect. I'll try to get my mom's car."

Samantha had just gotten Shining groomed and saddled when Mandy was dropped off at Whitebrook that afternoon by her mother. With her usual enthusiasm, Mandy scrambled from her mother's car and made her way to where Samantha was holding Shining's bridle.

"Look, Mama!" Mandy cried excitedly. "See how much better Shining looks? She and I are getting better together." Mandy went over to Shining, who lowered her head gently in anticipation of some loving pats.

"I see that, honey," Mrs. Jarvis said with a smile. She shook Samantha's hand. "Good to see you again. I'll be back around five o'clock to pick Mandy up if that's okay with you."

"She'll be ready," Samantha promised, and Mrs. Jarvis drove off to do some errands.

Samantha grinned at Mandy. "I have a surprise for you," she said lightly.

Mandy's soft chocolate-brown eyes grew wide.

"Are you going to ride Shining again, so I can watch?" Mandy asked breathlessly.

Samantha shook her head. "Nope," she said. "*You're* going to ride Shining so *I* can watch."

For a few startled moments Mandy only stared at Samantha. When she spoke, her voice was a squeak. "What?"

Shining had been coming along so well, and her behavior was so predictable and stable, that Samantha had decided it would be fine for the little girl to ride Shining—while Samantha led them around with a lead shank, of course. She'd hoped it would be a special treat for Mandy, and from the looks of things, it was.

"Do you mean it?" Mandy cried, gazing at Shining with adoring eyes.

"Yep. Let's get Len to help."

Two minutes later Len had lifted Mandy onto Shining's back, where she sat with perfect form deep in the saddle, shoulders straight. Her tiny legs in their heavy braces were well supported by the much-shortened stirrups, and her hands gripped a chunk of Shining's mane as well as the reins, for extra stability.

"Wow! What have we here?" Ashleigh called, a big smile on her face. "I think I see a future jockey!"

Mandy's smile couldn't have been any broader as she beamed at Samantha, Ashleigh, and Len. Holding tight with one hand, she used the other to pat Shining's neck. "I can't believe I'm riding you, girl," she said. "It's like Christmas and my birthday all at the same time!"

Holding Shining's shank, Samantha began to lead horse and rider around the stable yard at an easy pace. Shining's gait was smooth and even, and there was no way the little girl would become unseated, as long as she held on. Just to be on the safe side, though, Len walked casually on the other side, ready to spring into action if Mandy should lose her balance.

For her part, Mandy sat tall in the saddle, speechless with happiness. Ashleigh had run back to the farmhouse for her Polaroid camera, and now she took several pictures of Mandy proudly riding her favorite horse.

"I'm riding a real horse," Mandy said excitedly. "A racehorse! Wait till I tell the other Pony Commandos and my parents! Someday, when she starts winning races, I can say I rode her." She turned bright eyes to Samantha. "This was the best surprise, Sammy. I love Shining, and I love you!"

Samantha smiled at her, then turned away so Mandy wouldn't see the tears in her eyes. For ten minutes they walked around the yard and down along the driveway, until Samantha could see that Mandy was tiring. Len helped her down.

Instantly she turned to kiss Shining's nose. "Thank you, Shining. That was the best ride I ever had. I'll never forget it."

Then Mandy sat on a hay bale in the stable and chatted with Samantha while Samantha groomed Shining and fed her.

When Mrs. Jarvis returned, Mandy went to her,

clutching the snapshots Ashleigh had taken. "Mama! Mama! Look! This is me! This is me on Shining!"

Excitedly Mrs. Jarvis examined the photographs, then hugged Mandy in congratulations. "Honey, you look very professional," she said happily. "Daddy will be so proud. Let's hurry home and show him."

After Mandy was settled in the car, Mrs. Jarvis gave Samantha a hug. "You're our guardian angel, you know that?" she said softly.

"No one had more fun than I did," Samantha replied.

The next morning Samantha was all set to breeze Shining for the first time. Ashleigh had agreed to time them and was standing at the rail of the track when Samantha led Shining out. Ashleigh looked as anxious as Samantha felt.

"Morning, Ash."

"Morning. You sound stuffed up," Ashleigh said as she gave Samantha a leg into the saddle. "Are you coming down with something?"

Frowning, Samantha shook her head. "No, I'm probably just not awake yet." In truth, she wasn't feeling that great, but she figured a lot of it had to do with nervousness about that morning's work. It was an important moment.

"Are you set on what you're going to do?" Ashleigh asked.

Samantha settled into the saddle and collected the reins. "I'm going to gallop her through three quarters, then breeze her out the last quarter—and hope she'll change gears and kick in."

"I don't think you're going to have any problems," Ashleigh said, but Samantha thought she detected a touch of uncertainty in her voice. "Good luck."

Samantha urged Shining forward onto the track and took the filly through a warm-up lap at a trot and then a canter. She forced herself to relax. If Shining refused to kick in today, they would just keep working at it, but Samantha couldn't deny that she really had her hopes up.

As they passed Ashleigh and the mile marker pole for the first time, Samantha let Shining out into a relaxed gallop. The filly responded eagerly as she'd been doing in their last workouts. Samantha kept her in by the rail as they went around the first turn and down the backstretch. The only sounds in the morning air were Shining's rhythmic hoofbeats and snorted breaths. *So far, so good*, Samantha thought, but the test would come when she asked Shining to pick up the pace.

Going into the far turn, Samantha looked ahead to the quarter pole, marking the last quarter mile of the track. As she and Shining approached, she prepared herself, and as they came up to the marker, Samantha leaned farther over Shining's withers, clucked loudly, and kneaded her hands up the filly's neck.

For an instant Shining seemed to hesitate, then Samantha felt her gather her muscles. Suddenly they burst into a faster pace as Shining extended her stride. *All right!* Samantha thought.

As they came out of the far turn, Shining had accelerated into a fast, ground-eating gallop. Samantha almost let out a whoop of joy. This was perfect—perfect—better than she'd expected! They thundered past the eighth pole—only one furlong to go. Wind whipped Samantha's ponytail off her back and stung her eyes. Her heart was pounding in excitement, but she couldn't distinguish it from the pounding of Shining's hooves.

As they swept past the sixteenth pole, Samantha experimented and clucked to the filly again. With an exhilarating rush, Shining reached down and found even more power, churning them toward the finish. From her years of exercising horses, Samantha didn't need a stopwatch to know they were setting terrific fractions.

As they swept past the final pole, Samantha stood in her stirrups and began pulling Shining back into a canter. "Incredible!" she cried to the filly. "Good girl! I love you!"

Not since she'd last worked Pride in the fall had she ridden a horse through such a fast breeze. Shining arched her neck at Samantha's praise, and Samantha lovingly patted her neck. It was hard to believe that this was the same horse that had barely had the strength to lift her feet off the ground three months ago.

Ashleigh was grinning from ear to ear when they rode off the oval. Leaping off Shining's back, Samantha hugged the filly, then Ashleigh, laughing.

Ashleigh held up the stopwatch for Samantha's inspection. "Wow!" Samantha cried. "I knew we were making good fractions, but I didn't know they'd be that good!"

Len and Mike had come over from the training stable to watch and were grinning, too.

"Twenty-three seconds for the quarter!" Ashleigh exclaimed excitedly. "And she did the last furlong faster than the first! Amazing!" She grabbed Samantha again, and they danced in a little circle.

"Well, well," Mike said to Samantha. "It looks like you just may have a racehorse on your hands. Congratulations, Sammy. You've really worked wonders with her!"

Len nodded his agreement. "The little lady is turning into something special."

Samantha couldn't wait to tell Tor and Yvonne and Mandy. She knew they'd be as thrilled as she was.

"If she keeps training like this," Mike said, "she could be ready to go back to the races in about a month."

Samantha stared at him. "You think so?"

"There are never any guarantees in this business, but I wouldn't be surprised."

Samantha turned and took Shining's head in her hands. "Did you hear that, girl? Mike thinks you can race in a month. You *will* make it back to the track. I knew you would!"

"Sammy, I'm so happy for you," Tor said later that night, squeezing Samantha's hands over the table. They were at a little coffee shop in Lexington. "You made that happen today—no one else. You turned Shining into a real racehorse."

Samantha nodded and started to speak, but was interrupted by a sneeze. She blew her nose on a tissue from her purse.

"I can't imagine why she did so badly last summer," Samantha said when she could talk again. "It was obvious to me today that she loves to run. And she's not just good at it, she loves it. It must have been the way they were treating her." Her face creased into an angry frown. "I swear, if I ever get my hands on those idiots who trained her . . ."

"Look at it this way: winning races will be the best revenge. When those people see Shining in the winner's circle, they'll want to jump off a cliff," Tor assured her.

"Jumping's too good for them," Samantha said, then sneezed again.

Tor frowned. "You've been sneezing all evening, and you look flushed." Leaning over, he kissed Samantha's forehead. "Sammy! You're burning up. Why didn't you say something?"

"I feel okay," she insisted weakly. The truth was, she had been feeling worse and worse all day. But she, Tor, and Sierra were leaving for the 'chase in Aiken in the morning! She couldn't miss it.

"Come on." Tor stood up and put some bills on the table for their food. "Let's get you home."

"I thought we were going to go over Sierra's strategy for tomorrow," Samantha protested, reaching for her light jacket.

"Not with you in this shape. I don't even think you should go tomorrow."

"Tor, I have to!" Samantha cried. "It's Sierra's first steeplechase since last fall."

In the car, Tor considered. "Look," he said. "We have to leave at four o'clock tomorrow morning to get down to Aiken in time to have Sierra settled and relaxed for the 'chase at two o'clock. In the morning, when I come to get Sierra, we'll see how you're doing. But I don't think you'll be well enough to go. Maybe your dad or Mike will want to go with me."

"I'll be ready," Samantha insisted. "At four o'clock."

At four o'clock in the morning, however, Samantha was still in bed, glaring at her father over the thermometer in her mouth.

He took it out and peered at the numbers in the light of her bedside lamp. "I can never read these things," he muttered. "Ah! One hundred and one degrees. And two tenths. You're not going anywhere, young lady."

"But Dad—" Samantha's protest was interrupted by a bout of sneezing.

Wordlessly, her father handed her a fresh box of Kleenex. Ten minutes later, after leaving strict instructions that she was to stay in bed until their return on Sunday, Mr. McLean left with Tor in the small two-horse van. With a weary groan, Samantha rolled over and went back to sleep.

Later that morning Ashleigh stopped by with some fresh orange juice. "Lovely way to spend your weekend," she teased.

"How's Shining?" Samantha asked.

"Fine. She's much less shy around me now. In fact, she's completely fine around everyone at White-brook. It's only strangers she still doesn't like. Don't worry."

Eagerly, Samantha sat up on the couch where she had been curled up, watching TV. "Ash, I've been thinking. But tell me if you think it's crazy. What do you think about entering Shining in a maiden allowance race at Keeneland at the end of April?"

Sitting back in an easy chair, Ashleigh smiled. "Well, Mike thinks it's possible, and you know how much I respect his opinion."

"But do you think that would be pushing her too hard?" Samantha asked uncertainly.

"From what I saw yesterday, I think she's ready for a challenge," Ashleigh said. "Of course, she'll need more conditioning, but with regular workouts over the next month, I don't see that as a problem."

"You don't think yesterday's breeze was just a fluke?"

Ashleigh shook her head. "She wanted to run. She was doing it for you, Sammy, trying to please the first person who's shown her love and kindness. Anyway, we can breeze her again next week and find out for sure. If she turns in another fantastic performance, there's still plenty of time to enter her in the Keeneland race."

Samantha smiled, grateful for Ashleigh's experience and honest opinion. "That's exactly what we'll do. Thanks."

By that afternoon, Samantha had managed to shower and dress, and was sitting morosely in the kitchen looking at a bowl of canned chicken noodle soup.

The doorbell rang, and she sneezed at the same time.

Grabbing a tissue, she blew her nose as she answered the door.

Yvonne and Beth Raines were both on the doorstep.

"We ran into each other on the way in," Yvonne explained. "Any news from Tor?"

"Nope," Samantha said, motioning them to enter. They joined her in the kitchen as she opened a package of crackers to go with her soup. "The 'chase isn't televised, and I won't know anything until he calls me. But he should be getting ready about now," she added, looking at the clock.

"Here, try this," Beth said, holding out a plastic container. "Canned soup isn't the way to go when you're sick. This is homemade."

"Thanks!" she exclaimed. "I feel better already. It was so sweet of you guys to come see me. Sit down, but don't get too close."

Soon after lunch Beth left, and Samantha and Yvonne moved to the living room.

"I can't stand not being there," Samantha fretted, reaching for a tissue. She looked at the clock, wondering how Tor and Sierra were doing.

"It's a shame you got sick now," Yvonne sympathized. "But your dad will be able to help him. And you know Tor will call as soon as he can."

Yet it wasn't until almost four o'clock that the phone rang, and Samantha pounced on it.

"He won it!" Tor cried. "Sierra won it!"

"Oh, my gosh," Samantha gasped, sitting down on the sofa and waving at Yvonne. "I can't believe it! His first steeplechase since his injury, and he wins. Tell me everything!"

"I'm telling you, Sammy, it was a close call. In the middle of the second circuit, a horse went down right in front of us. I thought for sure we were goners. I didn't know how we could possibly get clear, but somehow, Sierra managed it. He changed his course in midjump and landed to one side. I've never seen such a smart horse. He's amazing! Sorry it took me so long to call you, but I had to wait for a free phone."

"Oh, Tor, I'm so happy for you—and Sierra. I just wish I hadn't let you down by being sick today."

"Sammy, don't be silly," Tor said firmly. "You could never let me down. And even though we both missed you today, your dad helped handle Sierra and everything was fine. Don't think any more about it. Listen, we want to finish getting Sierra settled. I'll call you later tonight from the hotel, and then I'll see you tomorrow. Okay?"

"Okay. I'm so glad you won, Tor. I'm so proud of you."

"Be proud of Sierra—he did all the work."

A few minutes later Yvonne had to go home. "I'm so thrilled about Tor and Sierra, Sammy. That's great news. Now you can just concentrate on getting better. Remember, we're supposed to go shopping Tuesday."

147

Samantha laughed. "I could be on my deathbed and you'd still drag me out to go shopping."

"You know it," Yvonne said.

After dinner Samantha was watching TV and thinking happily of Tor and Sierra's win, and of her own plans for Shining, when the doorbell rang again.

"Mr. and Mrs. Jarvis!" she cried in surprise when she opened the door. Mandy's parents were standing on her doorstep.

"Hello, Samantha," Mr. Jarvis said. "Please forgive us for dropping by unannounced. We were on our way to a movie in Lexington, and decided to stop by to see you on the spur of the moment."

"No, it's fine," Samantha said, opening the door wider. "Please come in. Can I get you anything?"

"No, no, thank you." Mr. and Mrs. Jarvis perched on the couch.

"We've come to talk to you about Mandy," Mrs. Jarvis began, casting a look at her husband.

"It's about her progress, in a way," he continued. "I can't tell you how excited we are about how well she's doing. In the last two months she's improved more than in the entire last year."

"I'm so glad," Samantha said. "I love spending time with her. She's a special girl."

"We think so, too," Mr. Jarvis said. "Which is why we're here. You know how horse-crazy our daughter is—more so now than ever. All she talks about at home are her riding lessons and her time at Whitebrook."

"Ever since you introduced her to Shining," Mrs.

Jarvis added, "she's taken a special interest in the horse. She relates to Shining, as someone who has been hurt and is on her way to making a comeback. For Mandy to have been a part of that comeback—" Mrs. Jarvis broke off, emotional tears welling up in her brown eyes.

Her husband took over. "What we're trying to say is that Shining is a very special horse to Mandy. Mandy has asked for a horse of her own for her birthday later this month, and we've agreed. Her own horse would be just the encouragement she needs to continue with her recovery."

"Samantha," Mrs. Jarvis said, a pleading note in her voice, "we've come to ask you to let us buy Shining—for Mandy."

12

FOR SEVERAL LONG MOMENTS SAMANTHA SAT THERE, dumbfounded and unable to speak. Sell Shining? Sell the first horse she ever owned? It had never crossed her mind—never. And to sell Shining now, when she finally seemed ready to race again?

"Uh, um, I don't know," she muttered, scrambling to get her thoughts into order.

"We know how special Shining is to you," Mrs. Jarvis said quickly. "We know it's a lot to ask."

"It's just that we feel so strongly that Shining is the key to Mandy's complete recovery. She's formed a bond with the horse."

So have I, thought Samantha numbly.

Mr. and Mrs. Jarvis looked at each other a little uncomfortably, obviously taken aback by Samantha's shocked reaction.

"I'm just surprised," Samantha said, trying to reassure them. "Selling Shining had never occurred to

151

me. She's the first horse I've ever owned."

"We know," Mrs. Jarvis said. "But we felt we had to at least ask. We'll understand if you want to keep Shining—we'll accept any decision you make. But we're willing to make a very generous offer. Perhaps you could buy another horse with the money—a better horse, even."

Samantha heaved a sigh. "I'll really have to think about it. I just don't know what to say right now. But tell me—would you consider racing Shining, if you bought her for Mandy?"

A small frown crossed Mr. Jarvis's face, and he shook his head reluctantly. "I'm afraid not. We can afford to buy Shining, and to keep her here at Whitebrook, stable fees, feed, vet bills, and so on. But there's no way we can take on the commitment of keeping her in training, the training fees, entry fees to races, jockey fees. We just couldn't."

Samantha was ready to cry out, "No!" Then she thought of Mandy and how totally thrilled the little girl would be if Shining were her own horse. "If it's okay with you, I'll need to think about it for a while. Mandy's birthday is at the end of the month, right?"

"April thirtieth," Mrs. Jarvis confirmed.

"I'll definitely make a decision soon," Samantha promised. Suddenly she felt her cold flaring up again. Her head pounded, she felt hot and feverish, and she could hardly breathe.

"Thank you," Mr. Jarvis said. "We know how difficult this is for you. We appreciate your considering it."

"Thank you," Mrs. Jarvis repeated, clasping

Samantha's hand. "Now we'll get out of your way so you can rest."

It seemed like hours that Samantha sat on the couch after the Jarvises left. The TV hummed in the background, but she neither saw nor heard it. Two words kept pounding through her head. *Sell Shining. Sell Shining. Sell Shining.*

Of course her first reaction was, *No way.* But to be fair, how could she just say no without giving the decision any thought? Suddenly she pictured Mandy riding Shining, but it was a different Mandy, a few years older. She sat tall and proud in the saddle, her back straight, her strong, healthy legs gripping Shining's sides. It was an image of what might be.

Sighing, Samantha got to her feet and clicked off the TV. One thing was for sure: she couldn't decide anything tonight, not the way she felt. In the kitchen she poured herself a glass of juice, then got some vitamin C and some Tylenol, and headed upstairs.

"They did what?" Tor's blue eyes widened in shock. He, Samantha, Gregg, and Yvonne had met at an Italian restaurant in Lexington to celebrate Tor's win. After kissing Tor and giving him firsthand congratulations on the win, she had told them all about the Jarvises' offer.

"They asked me to sell Shining," Samantha confirmed miserably, taking a sip of her milk shake.

Samantha's cold was much better, but her mental state had taken a turn for the worse. For the last two days she had done nothing but think over what the Jarvises had suggested. Instead of making things clearer, however, the more she thought about it, the more confused she became.

"Well, of course you told them no," Yvonne said, looking indignant.

Samantha shook her head. "I promised I'd think about it."

"What?" Yvonne shrieked. "Why on earth would you need to think about it? Of course you're not going to sell Shining—to them or anybody. It was crazy for them to ask you. Just tell them you're sorry, but you can't. They'll understand."

As Tor soothingly rubbed her arm, Samantha said, "That's just it. When they first asked, I thought, 'Of course not. No way.' But since then I've been thinking. Maybe Mandy actually needs Shining more than I do. I mean, I *want* Shining, I *love* her. But do I really *need* her—the way that Mandy does?"

Tor frowned. "I see what you mean. For Mandy, Shining is almost like medicine, like therapy, helping her get better. For you, Shining is more of an emotional satisfaction."

Nodding, Samantha said, "Right. The thought of anyone else owning Shining makes me feel sick. But am I just being selfish? It's true what the Jarvises said—I could buy another horse with the money."

"No, no, no!" Yvonne smacked her hand against the table. "I don't believe that you would be happy with just any horse. You need Shining just as much as Mandy does. It's Shining who's important to you.

You saved her, you made her healthy again. You have just as much of a bond with her, and more important, she has a bond with you."

Groaning, Samantha dropped her head into her hands. "But she has a bond with Mandy, too. I've told you how she responds to her. In some ways, it's like they were made for each other."

"But weren't you thinking about running her in the maiden at Keeneland in only three weeks?" Tor asked. "If Shining has the potential to be a good racer, shouldn't she be given the chance?"

"I thought so," Samantha admitted hesitantly.

"Well, if the Jarvises can't keep her as a racer, won't that be like not allowing Shining to fulfill her potential?" Tor continued.

"I don't know!" Samantha wailed. "What if her potential is really to help a little girl walk again?"

"What does Ashleigh say?" Gregg asked quietly.

"I haven't told her yet," Samantha said. "I was in shock. But when we breeze Shining tomorrow, I'll tell her first thing."

"Let's try her at four furlongs today," Ashleigh suggested, walking into the oval early the next morning, stopwatch in hand.

"Will do." Samantha swung up into Shining's saddle, feeling the eager anticipation in the horse's body.

Today they would breeze out half a mile instead of just a quarter. Samantha couldn't breeze Shining every day—it would take too much out of the filly. She interspersed the breezes with slow, stamina-building gallops. If Shining did well today, though, Samantha could legitimately enter her in the end-of-April race at Keeneland. Of course, Samantha thought, feeling her heart contract, this might all become unnecessary—if she sold Shining to the Jarvises.

As Samantha warmed up Shining at a trot and then a canter around the training oval, she thought about how she would tell Ashleigh of the Jarvises' offer. After all, Ashleigh and Mike had given Shining to Samantha for free—would their feelings be hurt if she sold her? Would they understand how much Mandy seemed to need her?

"Sammy!" Ashleigh called. "What are you doing?"

Ashleigh's call snapped Samantha out of her musing. "Sorry. My mind wandered for a second." She realized she'd stopped Shining in the middle of the track.

"Are you okay?"

Samantha nodded. "I'm fine. Let's get started."

Len had rolled the three-stall practice starting gate across the track. Samantha urged Shining into the first slot.

Ashleigh looked at the stopwatch and held one hand in the air. Samantha watched her out of the corner of her eye. When Ashleigh suddenly dropped her hand, Len opened the gate. Samantha gave Shining rein, clicked her tongue, and yelled, "Go, girl!"

Instantly the Thoroughbred responded. Long days of painstaking practice had ensured that the filly knew every signal, and now she leaped immediately into a smooth, long-strided gallop. Despite her mental torment, Samantha couldn't help smiling as her horse left the gate far behind and roared around the oval. At the half-mile post, Samantha loosened her hold on the reins and asked for more speed. As before, the filly responded. Shining's muscles bunched and gathered in perfect rhythm as she pounded around the track.

Galloping was Samantha's favorite gait: on a good horse it was so smooth, so effortless, it felt like flying. She could barely feel Shining's hooves hitting the dirt beneath them. The wind on her face and the sight of Shining's mane whipping back with the speed of her gallop were exhilarating. For long moments Samantha heard nothing but the mingled thud of hoofbeats and heartbeats, felt nothing but the machinelike pumping of the Thoroughbred beneath her, saw nothing but dirt track between Shining's two alert pointed ears, flicked back to listen for any command from Samantha. She was repeating the fantastic performance she'd put in during her first breeze. Samantha knew that she could be ready for the Keeneland race.

If I sell her, she can't race. I can still ride her. I can still feed her, groom her, love her. I just can't train her. Or race her.

Before she realized it, they were flashing past the finish. Then Samantha stood in the stirrups, easing back slowly on the reins and calling, "Easy, girl, easy. Good girl, good Shining."

After Shining dropped into a comfortable trot, not winded in the least, Samantha turned her and headed back to where Ashleigh was grinning and waving the stopwatch.

"That was incredible! Your second quarter was faster than the first!" she crowed, making such a ruckus that Mike and Len came running from the training barn. "Forty-six and a half seconds! We've got a racehorse!"

Involuntary tears sprang to Samantha's eyes as she took in what Ashleigh was saying.

"Sammy, what's wrong?" Ashleigh took Shining's bridle so Samantha could dismount. "I knew you shouldn't ride today!" she exclaimed. "You're still sick."

"No, I'm not," Samantha protested. Then, without warning, she burst into tears. Mike, Len, and Ashleigh all exchanged puzzled glances and crowded around Samantha. Mike took Shining's bridle so Ashleigh could put her arms around the younger girl.

Finally, through sobs, Samantha recounted the Jarvises' offer to buy Shining—to buy *her* horse, who now was showing so much potential as a racer. Len offered to walk Shining and cool her down, and Ashleigh led Samantha back to the McLean cottage for a good talk.

"So what did Ashleigh and Mike say?" Yvonne asked, dipping a French fry in a pool of ketchup. The girls had stopped for a snack at the food court before hitting the rest of the mall.

"They were really nice about it," Samantha told her. "First they said that what I do with Shining is

158

completely up to me, and if I wanted to sell her, I could. And they said they understood why it was a difficult decision. Obviously, if it was anyone besides Mandy, I could immediately say no and not think twice about it. But because it *is* Mandy, everything's different. I really care about her. I would give almost anything to help her get better. I just don't know if I can give her the *main* thing. Does that make me selfish?" Samantha brushed her hair back over her shoulder and took a deep breath.

"I care about Mandy, too, and all the other Pony Commandos," Yvonne said earnestly, leaning forward on the table. "And I know you have a special relationship with her. But that doesn't mean you have to give up your own dreams. Tell the Jarvises to get her another horse, a smaller one that's easier for her to ride. A big pony."

"Ugh, I'm sick of thinking about it," Samantha said. "It's all I've been doing. Let's talk about something else."

"Okay." Yvonne's almond-shaped black eyes sparkled. "Let's talk about how I'm going to Florida with Gregg once school is out this summer."

Samantha stared at Yvonne. "What?" she finally managed.

Laughing, Yvonne said, "With him and his *family*, dummy. They're renting a house in Florida for a week, and they've invited me. I can share a room with his sister, Tina. I can't wait—it's going to be right on the beach."

"Wow!" Samantha said, breaking off a piece of her

chocolate-chip cookie. "Family vacations. Going away together. Next thing I know you'll be announcing your engagement."

"No way!" Yvonne said with a smile. "I adore Gregg, and I love dating him, but I still have to go to college and maybe graduate school. I don't want to get married till I'm at least twenty-five. I even think Ashleigh got married a little young, although she and Mike are perfect for each other. But she's only twenty-two, and Mike was really her only boyfriend."

"Yeah, but you know they were made for each other. Why wait if you're in love?"

The two friends argued good-naturedly for a few minutes, finally agreeing to disagree. Then Yvonne cheerfully dragged Samantha to her favorite clothing store, which Samantha had never ventured into before.

"Here, try this on," Yvonne advised half an hour later, holding up a knit top. "This would be a good color on you."

Samantha glumly took the shirt and headed into a dressing cubicle. Never an enthusiastic shopper, she was feeling so low today that all she could do was follow Yvonne's instructions mindlessly. So far Yvonne had already fixed her up with two new pairs of leggings with big matching T-shirts, and a pair of flowered shorts. Looking down at her ragged jeans, she had to acknowledge that she could use some new clothes. But she would much prefer to be spending her hard-earned money on something interesting, like new tack, or perhaps a pair of jodhpurs.

Her friend was waiting for her when she came out.

Frowning, she regarded Samantha critically, then smiled and nodded. "Yep. We'll take it. It'll be cute with jeans or a denim skirt, and it matches both pairs of leggings."

Samantha couldn't help smiling. "I think you've found your dream job, Yvonne. I'm sure they'd hire you here if you were interested." Turning, she headed back into the dressing room to change.

"Samantha, believe me, you need some new clothes. You may not have grown since you were fifteen, but I bet you haven't *shopped* since then, either. And it's not my fault you have zero fashion sense."

Inside the changing cubicle, Samantha giggled. What Yvonne said was true. For some reason, she could pore over saddle and other tack catalogs by the hour, dreaming of this saddle and that bridle and those riding boots. But regular everyday clothes seemed intensely boring. She wondered if Tor minded how little she paid attention to her wardrobe. Sighing, she figured that he didn't care any more than she did.

"Look at this great dress!" Yvonne was holding up a black Lycra minidress. "I'm going to get it. Do you want to look at anything else?"

Samantha groaned. "Noooo. I'm shopped out. Please, let's go home."

"Not yet," Yvonne insisted. "We haven't looked at any shoes." Samantha groaned again.

The rest of the week seemed to fly by for Samantha, but she was still no closer to making a decision about Shining and Mandy. On Saturday morning, she approached Pride's stall brimming with emotion. It was to be their first ride together since Pride's return from the clinic.

"Hello, Pride," Samantha crooned to the big horse, who was stamping impatiently in his stall. "You want to go for a little ride?"

Pride whoofed out his breath, as though to say, "About time! I've been waiting."

Samantha gave a little smile, then rubbed his beautiful head and hugged him. "Come on, then. Let's get you tacked up."

Leading Pride out into the stable yard, Samantha decided that it really felt like spring. Warm sunshine coated everything with a golden glow, spring flowers were pushing up everywhere, and in the pastures, heavy banks of sweet-smelling clover waved over the small hills.

Out in the stable yard Ashleigh waited with Shining, who was also tacked up. Knowing that Samantha hadn't come to any decision yet, Ashleigh had suggested that she ride Shining. If Samantha was going to race the horse, then it was understood that Ashleigh would jockey the filly. The better she got to know Shining, the better their chances in any race.

Ashleigh swung up on Shining and Samantha mounted Pride. It was like old times, she thought, remembering the countless hours she had exercise ridden Wonder's Pride while he was in training. Now, although the big horse wasn't racing anymore, he still needed to be kept in top condition.

At first Shining seemed surprised, but not fearful

of having Ashleigh on her back. With the slightest look to her left she could see Samantha, and that seemed to reassure her.

"She's doing great," Ashleigh said as they trotted slowly over the dirt trail.

Samantha nodded.

Ashleigh looked over in concern. "Thinking about selling Shining is getting to you, isn't it?"

"Yes," Samantha said miserably. "But I'm seeing the Pony Commandos tomorrow at Tor's. Maybe that'll help make up my mind."

"Mandy's terrific—a kid in a million." Ashleigh spoke Samantha's unsaid thoughts. Then, sensing Samantha's emotional torment, she changed the subject. "How does Pride seem? He sure looks glad to be back."

At that Samantha smiled and lovingly rubbed a hand down Pride's shoulder. "It feels great to be riding him again." Pride snorted happily and arched his neck. "You're right. He's definitely happy to be home."

"Mr. Townsend and I are getting dozens of inquiries about him," Ashleigh told her. "The stud fees will really come in handy. Mike and I are thinking of having the barns painted, and of redoing the kitchen at the farmhouse."

As they reached a wide straight lane, they exchanged a look. Then each young woman clucked her tongue, hunched over her horse's withers, and kneaded her hands along her mount's neck. Pride and Shining, needing no further urging, leaped out into an easy, smooth-gaited gallop, running companionably side by side along the dirt trail.

This is ecstasy, Samantha thought as they thundered down familiar trails. *If only it could stay like this. If only nothing had to change.*

13

"SO HOW ARE YOU, SAMMY?" TOR PUT AN ARM AROUND
Samantha's shoulders and gave her a light kiss on the
forehead. They were at Tor's stable, setting up cavallettis and a couple of other very low poles for the
Pony Commandos to step their mounts over.

"I'm okay," Samantha replied, her green eyes filled
with confusion.

"Made any decisions yet?"

"Nothing definite. I'm leaning toward keeping
Shining," she admitted, "but I wanted to see Mandy
today. Maybe that'll help me make up my mind."

"Good idea. When do you have to decide?"

"Mandy's birthday is on the thirtieth; the Keeneland race is on the twenty-ninth. If I want to enter
Shining, I have until the twenty-third, as long as I pay
a late fee. So I have about two more weeks."
Samantha frowned as she shifted a white-painted
pole a little with her foot. "But I'll probably decide

before then—I couldn't take two more weeks of this. I'm going to get an ulcer."

"Poor baby," Tor sympathized. "You know that whatever you decide, I'll support you."

Samantha gave him a grateful smile. "Thanks."

"Sammy! Sammy!" Mandy Jarvis made her way as quickly as she could over to Samantha.

The older girl greeted her with a hug and a big smile. "Hi! What's up?"

"Mama and Daddy said yes! They're going to get me my own horse for my birthday!"

Samantha pretended great surprise. "Really? That's terrific, Mandy. I bet you're excited."

"I am! I don't know how I'll ever wait that long. Did you know I'll be seven years old?" Clearly Mandy was impressed by her own advanced age.

"Wow, seven, huh? That's a good age to get your first horse," Samantha said, helping Mandy into Butterball's saddle. Firmly she pushed down thoughts of how old she was when she got *her* first horse—and how short a time she might have her.

Mandy nodded vigorously. "I think so, too. How's Shining?"

"She's fine. Her morning workouts have been terrific—it's incredible."

A smile lit Mandy's delicate face. "So she's going to race again?" she said excitedly.

"I'm not sure," Samantha said slowly.

"But Sammy, I think she wants to race again!" Mandy cried. "You have to let her!"

166

Samantha smiled at the little girl's enthusiasm. "We'll see, Mandy. There are a lot of different things she could do. Racing is just one of them."

Mandy frowned. "What could be better than racing?"

Laughing, Samantha said, "Don't let Tor hear you say that—he thinks jumping is the best!"

"Okay, Commandos!" Tor clapped from across the oval. "First, I want everyone to warm up his or her pony by walking in a circle. Then we'll try trotting. Later, we have some low jumps set up. Everybody ready?"

Six excited children yelled, "Yes!"

In reality, the "jumps" were only about four inches off the ground, low poles that even the fattest pony could easily trot over without risking losing its rider. But, to the Pony Commandos, Samantha knew that jumping seemed incredibly daring.

As usual, Samantha led Butterball and Mandy, while Tor, Yvonne, Gregg, Beth, and Janet led the others. Every once in a while Samantha looked back at Mandy's happy face, her excited smile, and her carefully correct posture. The little girl's obvious pleasure in riding, and the freedom and mobility it gave her, constricted Samantha's heart painfully.

Mandy and Shining were two of a kind. Each could help the other. Samantha, with her health and natural athletic ability, could empathize with both the abused horse and the injured child, but that was all. When Mandy looked at Shining, she really *knew* what Shining felt. It was true that if Samantha sold Shining to Mandy, the filly would probably never race, even though she had incredible potential. But it was also true that if she did become a champion racer, she might never fulfill one sweet, fragile, damaged little girl's dream. And who was to say that *that* destiny wasn't the most important? With a sudden lump in her throat, Samantha was certain she finally knew what she had to do.

In the meantime, however, there was a lesson to get through. The Commandos loved the new challenge of the small jumps and fearlessly met them head-on, calling encouragement to their good-natured mounts. One after another, the fat little ponies trotted over the low poles, causing their riders to whoop with joy and excitement.

After the lesson, Tor gave a brief talk about horse care. The Commandos listened in rapture, dreaming of the day when they would be able to groom their ponies themselves.

Then Mr. Jarvis came to pick up his daughter, and he smiled and shook Samantha's hand, giving her no impression of impatience about her decision.

"Daddy, guess what Butterball did today?" Mandy cried happily. With a final wave at Samantha, she walked clumsily beside her father, chattering the whole way. "Butterball's so smart, Daddy. And you know what else?" Gradually her thin, high voice faded as they walked through the door of the stable out to the parking lot.

"Good lesson, everyone!" Beth called cheerfully. "Many thanks for your help. See you here in two weeks for some more Commando action!" After gathering up her purse and light sweater, Beth gave a wave and headed out to her own car.

Automatically Samantha started to clear out the props from the pony lesson. Tomorrow Tor would be giving an advanced jumping lesson, and she usually helped him set up for it. While she and Tor arranged the jumps with quiet teamwork, her mind was humming with the implications of the decision she'd come to. Of course, Shining would stay at White-brook. *But what if the Jarvises move?* Samantha would be able to feed and groom and even exercise ride Shining almost every day. *Until Mandy improves enough and is old enough to do it herself.* She would be able to see Mandy's progress firsthand, as the little girl, inspired by her very own horse, grew better and better—perhaps she might even walk again one day unaided. *But you won't ever see Shining race.*

Setting her jaw, Samantha shifted the pieces of one large jump into position. She couldn't think about it anymore. Her mind was made up, and she knew what she had to do.

That night Samantha and her father had dinner at the main farmhouse with Mike, Ashleigh, and Mr. Reese. They sat in silence through most of the meal, as though everyone could sense Samantha's preoccupation.

Finally, as Ashleigh was slicing thick pieces of homemade pound cake, Samantha said in a small voice, "I've made my decision."

The cake knife clattered to the table, but Ashleigh

quickly snatched it up again. No one pretended not to know what Samantha was talking about.

Looking up, Samantha met her father's eyes. "I've decided to—" Her voice cracked, and she coughed to disguise it. "I've decided that Mandy needs Shining more than I do."

Then she sat miserably in her chair, her head bowed, her fingers nervously ripping her paper napkin to shreds.

Ashleigh sat down in her own chair with a thump, her hazel eyes wide, yet filled with compassion and understanding. She reached out and covered one of Samantha's hands with her own.

"Oh, Sammy," she breathed. "What a decision. It's very brave of you, but are you sure?"

Nodding, Samantha whispered, "Yes. They really need each other."

"Don't you think Shining needs you, too?" Mr. McLean asked.

"Not as much as Mandy needs her," Samantha said.

"I understand," Ashleigh said. "I thought you might do this. Well, if you're sure, I know you're going to make one little girl *very* happy."

Grateful for her support, Samantha smiled at Ashleigh through unshed tears. Then she pushed back her chair and said, "Please excuse me. I have to go see Shining."

No one said a word as she left. Outside, the air was clear and cool, still tinged with the fresh scents of a bright, sunny day. In spite of the pain Samantha felt, she also felt a measure of relief. The decision was made. She didn't have to think about it anymore.

Inside the mares' barn, Samantha was comforted by the familiar stable smells of fresh hay, horses, and leather. Quietly Samantha greeted Wonder, Fleet Goddess, and then Shining.

Hearing Samantha's stride, Shining had come to the front of her stall and pushed her head over the top of the door. As usual, the kittens Midnight and Flurry played close by, attended by Snowshoe, who was contentedly washing one paw.

"Hey, girl," Samantha said, gently rubbing her hand over Shining's velvet nose. She took a carrot from her pocket and broke it into pieces, which the filly lipped up eagerly. Samantha felt a rush of love for Shining, for her strength, her courage, her refusal to give up even when her life must have been unbearable. Samantha also felt pride that her own love and faith had helped the filly become a beautiful, elegant example of horse breeding at its finest. She was grateful that she'd had the chance to do it.

"Oh, Shining, I have something to tell you," Samantha said, and it was only then that she felt the salty sting of tears fill her eyes. Keeping her voice low so it wouldn't break, she said, "You know how much Mandy loves you and needs you. And I know how much you love her. So she's going to be your owner soon, not me. I love you, and I love having you be my horse, but I think she needs you more. She's been hurt badly, Shining, and so have you. You two are good for each other. I know you can help her, and I think she can help you. Do you understand?"

The filly pushed her head out farther and gently lipped at Samantha's sweater. Then she butted Samantha very softly. The show of affection was more than Samantha could bear, and she began to cry. "Oh, Shining, what if she takes you away? What if you leave and I never see you again? How will I ever know if you could have succeeded as a racehorse? Am I doing the right thing?" Throwing her arms around her horse's neck, Samantha sobbed into the gleaming coat covering the solid, toned muscle. Shining stood patiently, letting Samantha cry against her, every so often nuzzling Samantha's curls with her nose. For long minutes Samantha cried, letting out all the anguish that she had been keeping inside ever since the Jarvises had approached her about Shining.

Finally a determined scuffling and scraping around her feet made her look down. A piece of hay was sticking up between her boots, and Flurry was attacking it viciously, first sneaking up, then pouncing with all her kitten might. From one extreme of emotion Samantha went to another, because she couldn't help giggling at the tiny cat's antics. Picking up the gray kitten, she rubbed its soft fur.

"Thanks, Flurry, for making me laugh. Say hello to Shining."

Carefully she held the kitten at eye level with the filly, and the two animals regarded each other seriously. Then Shining cautiously leaned out her nose, and Flurry just as cautiously patted it with one small paw, keeping her claws well sheathed. Samantha laughed again and put the kitten down on a hay bale. Then she dug in her pocket for a tissue and blew her nose.

"I'll get used to it, girl. It'll take a while, but I'll be okay. You will, too."

"Samantha? Sammy? You in there?"

Her father's voice made her quickly wipe her eyes against her sleeve.

"Here, Dad. By Shining."

"Honey, there's a phone call for you. It's the Jarvises." Her father's sympathetic face told her that he knew she'd been crying, and why, and that he understood.

Squaring her shoulders, Samantha said, "Okay. I'll go take it." Then she headed out into the night air toward the cottage.

"Hello, Samantha?"

"Hi, Mrs. Jarvis. I was going to call you tonight." Samantha swallowed hard, then cleared her throat so her voice would sound normal. This was the easy part—telling them that she had decided to sell them Shining. Making the decision had been hard; everything else from now on would never be as bad.

"Yes, well, I thought it best that we call you first," Mrs. Jarvis said. "You see, dear—we've been thinking. In the past few days Mandy has talked of nothing else but her hopes of seeing Shining race again. So much so that we've realized that just her looking forward to it might mean more to her than actually owning Shining herself."

173

There was a weird buzzing noise in Samantha's head. Clumsily she gripped the edge of the table and lowered herself into a chair. She was dimly aware of her father coming to stand beside her.

"What—what are you saying?"

"Mandy loves Shining," Mrs. Jarvis continued. "But one of the things she loves most about her is that she's a racehorse. For Mandy, the thought of Shining competing in a race—against all odds—is a very powerful motivator. We know that we could never keep up with all the fees and training that Shining would need to race. So, after a lot of heartfelt talking, we've decided that it would be best if Shining stayed with you."

"Really?" Samantha barely recognized her own voice. *I must be dreaming,* she thought.

"Yes. Not only that, but we've also realized how impractical it would be to get Mandy a full-size horse right now anyway. She's so young, and she's small for her age. After talking to Tor and Beth Raines, we've decided that a medium-size pony, like Butterball, would be best for her. In fact, just this evening Tor has offered Butterball to us, and we could board him at Tor's stables. So you see, everything has worked out for the best."

Samantha let out a huge sigh. "It does sound like you've made the best decision. And I'm thrilled to keep Shining—in fact, there's a race at the end of the month that I wanted to put her in. I know! The race is on the twenty-ninth. Please let Mandy come with me. It would be my birthday present to her."

"Oh, she would love that! And then on the following day, we'll have a party at Tor's stable for all the Commandos. Thank you, Samantha, for your generosity. Your friendship means so much to Mandy— and to us."

"She means a lot to me, too," Samantha said. "Remind her that I'm picking her up on Wednesday to bring her to Whitebrook. She can watch Shining train for the race."

"She'll be ready," Mrs. Jarvis promised.

After Samantha hung up, it took a full minute for the reality to sink in. Then she let out a whoop and jumped up to hug her father.

"Dad! They don't want Shining! They're getting a pony! I can keep her! I can keep her!" For the second time that day, tears flowed down Samantha's face, but this time they were tears of joy and relief.

14

MR. MCLEAN AND SAMANTHA DROVE UP TO THE JARVISES'
house at eight o'clock in the morning. It was the day
of the Keeneland race, and Mr. McLean had allowed
Samantha to take the day off from school. After all, it
wasn't every day that her own horse was racing at
Keeneland!

Shining was already at the track. They'd vanned
her over two days before so that Samantha could get
in a workout over the Keeneland track. Shining had
worked beautifully, and Samantha was feeling optimistic but nervous.

Their car came to a stop, and almost immediately
the Jarvises' front door was yanked open. Mandy
stood there, a grin practically splitting her face in two.
She was in her Sunday best, a beautiful floral-print
dress with a wide lace collar and puffed sleeves edged
with lace. A matching bow was nestled in her head of
dark curls, and she had a matching pocketbook as

well. She made such a charming picture that Samantha hardly noticed the heavy metal braces almost covered by her dress.

Samantha opened her door and jumped out. "Ready?"

"Ready as anything," Mandy declared, already making her way to the car. Mrs. Jarvis appeared behind her.

"She's been so excited," she told Samantha happily. "I don't think she slept a wink last night."

"That makes two of us," Samantha said wryly.

"My husband, Randall, and I are going to head to the race in a little while," Mrs. Jarvis said. "We wouldn't miss it for the world." She glanced over Samantha's shoulder to see Mr. McLean lifting Mandy up into the car. "Then we have to head over to Tor's to decorate for tomorrow's party. Randall's been blowing up balloons in the attic since daybreak." She hid a laugh behind her hand. "Thank you again for everything, Samantha."

"It's been my pleasure," Samantha said honestly. "Now I better get going so I can give Mandy a tour of the backside before the race. We'll see you there."

Mrs. Jarvis quickly kissed Mandy good-bye, and Samantha hopped back in the truck.

It didn't take long to reach Keeneland, since it was right in Lexington. Once there, Samantha checked Shining. The filly whickered a happy greeting. Samantha was relieved to see that the filly seemed relaxed and content. She'd been afraid the track might bring back unpleasant memories for Shining, but so far, so good.

Inside the stall, Mandy sat on a folding lawn chair as Samantha carefully groomed Shining for the most important day of her life.

"Hey, beautiful," Tor's voice said over the half-door of the stall. He looked over the door and saw Mandy. "And beautiful," he said to her with a grin. "And beautiful," he added to Shining, obviously not willing to leave any female out of the compliment.

Laughing, Samantha kissed him hello. "Did you find our seats?"

"Clubhouse seats, looking right down on the finish line." Shining was running in the third race, a maiden allowance race for three-year-old fillies that went off at two o'clock.

"My parents are coming, too," Mandy informed him.

"Shining is going to have more cheerleaders than any horse in the field," Tor told her. "Of course, I'm going to be cheering for the trainer." He gave Samantha a meaningful look, and she hugged him, leaning over the door, still holding a rag and a large finishing brush.

"Thank you," she said softly. "You've always stood by me—I couldn't have done it without you."

"Sure you could," Tor said firmly. "And don't you forget it. Of course, you might not have had as much fun doing it, but . . ."

"Oh, you!" Samantha left him and went back to smoothing Shining's healthy, glowing roan coat.

Tor laughed and winked at Mandy, who grinned back.

"Listen, ladies," he said. "I'm going to go get a hot dog. Do you guys want anything?"

179

Samantha's green eyes widened. "Tor, it's nine o'clock in the morning," she protested.

"Well, I'm starved. How about it? Hot dogs all around?"

"I'll take one," Mandy said instantly. "I was too excited to eat this morning."

Samantha gave in, a small rumble of her stomach reminding her that she'd been too nervous to eat also. "A little mustard, no chili."

"Be right back," Tor promised.

Finally it was time for Shining to go into the walking ring. She had been thoroughly groomed, and her mane and tail had been combed until they flowed like silk.

Mandy had headed to the grandstands to join Tor, Yvonne, Gregg, Mr. Reese, Mike, and Mr. McLean in what Tor referred to as the Shining Cheering Section. Now it was just Samantha, Shining, and Ashleigh, and the race was about to begin.

"Can you believe this?" Samantha asked Ashleigh, a joyful glow lighting her face.

Ashleigh shook her head happily. "I'm so proud of you, Sammy—of both of you." Ashleigh looked professional in the blue-and-white silks of Whitebrook Farms, and her hair was pulled back in a tight French braid.

For the last two weeks, ever since the Jarvises had withdrawn their offer to buy Shining, Samantha and Ashleigh had been working her, aiming her toward this race. The horse seemed to love running more each day and had set terrific times during her breezes. Ashleigh had been riding the filly, getting her used to a new jockey. Now the day had come, and the two young women knew they were as ready as they'd ever be.

"Remember," Ashleigh said, "Shining hasn't raced in a long time. I know she's trained well, but there's no guarantee she'll do well, much less win."

"I know," Samantha said. "For me it's enough that she's here at all. Did you see her odds?"

Ashleigh nodded. "Fifty to one. Looks like people remember her from last summer."

"They'll be seeing a different horse," Samantha said loyally. "A horse who's been loved and cared for." Samantha glanced over at the outside rail of the walking ring.

"Oh, no—look who's here," she said to Ashleigh. The unwelcome sight of Brad Townsend made Samantha frown slightly. She'd seen in the program that Her Majesty was running in a race later on the card. But with Brad and Lavinia watching Shining's race, Samantha felt even more of a need for Shining to do well. She didn't want the filly to embarrass herself with them looking on. *But she won't!* Samantha told herself.

Then the call came for jockeys to mount. Samantha gave Ashleigh a leg into the small racing saddle and walked her and Shining another circuit around the ring. Ashleigh reached down and squeezed Samantha's hand. "We'll do our best, Sammy."

Samantha allowed herself one last pat on Shining's

nose. "I believe in you, girl, and I love you, no matter what." She gave Ashleigh a quick glance. "I'll see you later," was all she could manage, and Ashleigh nodded. Then they were gone.

Her hands trembling with excitement, Samantha made her way to the stands and sat between Mandy and Tor. Tor took her hand and patted it, then draped his arm across the back of her seat.

Mandy was anxiously sitting on the edge of her seat, her warm brown eyes glued to the gate where the horses were being loaded.

"Shining is number five," she noted, then turned to Samantha. "Is that good?"

"I actually don't know," Samantha admitted. "I never saw her race before, so I don't know if she likes the inside or outside or middle of the track. But it isn't a bad spot, at any rate."

Perched on the edge of her seat, Samantha thought she had never felt so nervous—not even when Pride was racing in the Breeders' Cup. This was *her* horse running—her name was beside Shining's in the program. There might never be another day like it as long as she lived. She only hoped that Shining gave it a real effort. It didn't matter if the filly won or not— as long as she didn't just give up now, after she had come so far.

"And they're off!" the announcer suddenly cried into his microphone. The starting gate doors had swung open split seconds before, and with a collective surge, the horses broke out of their gates and began thundering down the track. It was a short race, only six furlongs, and Samantha knew Shining could cover the distance easily and in good time on the training oval. But she hadn't raced against so many other horses in almost a year.

"Fidelio takes the early lead," the announcer cried. "Cup o' Java is up in second . . . Dutch Baby is in third. The long shot, Shining, is back in the five spot. And as they pass the first quarter mile, we have—"

Samantha's heart was in her throat. Shining had never finished better than fourth in any of her past races, although Samantha knew now that the filly was capable of more. But would Shining perform, or would she stick with her old racing style and hang back in the middle of the pack?

Tor sensed Samantha's anxiety. "Shh," he soothed, his eyes still on the track. "Have faith."

"I'm trying," Samantha said tightly. Shining was still in fifth as the field pounded down the backstretch toward the far turn. Ashleigh had Shining clear on the outside. Samantha knew that Ashleigh wouldn't ask the filly to run until they were into the turn. She just prayed Shining would kick in.

"And as they go into the far turn," the announcer called, "Fidelio is holding on to the lead, then Cup o' Java, Dutch Baby . . . and the long shot, Shining, is starting to make a move. She's changed gears and is moving up on the outside into fourth—"

The announcer sounded amazed at Shining's burst of speed, but Samantha felt her heart leap with joy. Shining was running like she had on the Whitebrook training oval! She'd put behind her the old bad memories of the track.

"Yes!" Tor shouted as Shining continued to gain on the outside. She was up on the flank of Dutch Baby.

"Come on, girl!" Samantha cried. "You can do it! Go, Shining, go!"

All of them were calling out encouragement. Samantha could barely breathe as she watched Ashleigh and Shining continue to gain. They were up alongside Dutch Baby, and they were flying! The two leaders were only another length in front.

"She can do it, Tor," Samantha said with a gasp. "She can do it!"

"I told you to have faith!" Tor said with a grin. "That's the way, Shining!"

Then suddenly, halfway through the turn, Dutch Baby lunged out, bumping into Shining and forcing her out into the middle of the track. Dutch Baby's jockey pulled hard on his left rein, urging his filly back on course. It was clear that the bump had startled Shining and knocked her off stride.

Samantha felt sick. "That's done it. I don't know how she can come back to win it now."

Tor took her hand and squeezed it. Both of them watched silently as Shining valiantly tried to recover her momentum. Dutch Baby was now a length in front, although Samantha knew Dutch Baby would be disqualified for interference. Fidelio was still in the lead, and as they hit the top of the stretch, she started pulling away from the field. Samantha groaned. It didn't look as though any of the other fillies would be able to catch Fidelio, and Shining was back in fourth again.

But to her delight, Samantha saw that Shining was trying. The filly was in full stride again and coming on like a rocket! In seconds she made up her lost ground, moving up to pass Dutch Baby, then surging after the two leaders. "Go, girl!" Samantha shrieked. "That's the way! You're wonderful! Go get them!"

Tor still held Samantha's hand, but now he was gripping it painfully in excitement. "She's showing she's got heart, all right!" he cried.

"And down the stretch they come!" shouted the announcer. "After being bumped and checked on the far turn, Shining is back in gear again. This filly is moving! We could see a real upset here! This long shot has come out of nowhere to be a serious contender. At the eight pole Fidelio is holding on to a two-length lead, but Ashleigh Griffen has Shining in hot pursuit. They're up into second . . . cutting into Fidelio's lead with every stride!"

Samantha was on her feet, barely believing her eyes as Ashleigh and Shining moved up alongside Fidelio—then swept right on by the other filly. "She's going to win it, Tor! She's going to win it!"

The next few seconds seemed like a hazy dream to Samantha. No longer could she hear the announcer's commentary, or the amazed gasps and cheers of everyone around her. Tor was methodically pounding her back in unknowing excitement, but Samantha was hardly aware of it. She was only aware of Shining's slim, powerful legs leaping forward with huge strides. Then Samantha watched, a dazed smile on her face, as Shining and Ashleigh pulled farther out to the front and then crossed the finish line with a three-length lead! Fidelio was in second place, Cup o' Java was in third, and Dutch Baby was back in sixth. Shining had won!

Then suddenly tears were streaming down Samantha's face, and she was standing and cheering and screaming. Mandy was yelling, too, and Samantha picked her up and swung her around, laughing. She and Tor sandwiched Mandy between them and gave her a huge double hug.

Yvonne was shrieking, "She won! She won! My friend's horse won!" to anyone who would listen, and Gregg was hugging Yvonne and pumping Tor's hand.

On the track Ashleigh stood in the saddle in victory, waving up at the stands. Looking out at her friend, who had guided Shining through months of careful reconditioning and training, Samantha felt the tears start all over again.

And Shining. Shining was prancing proudly, seeming to know how well she had done, seeming to know she was a winner today for the first time in her life. Her feet rose high, her neck was arched, her elegant hindquarters danced over the dirt track. Samantha's heart almost burst with love and pride as she remembered the thin, listless, bedraggled filly who had arrived at Whitebrook on a chilly winter morning not long before.

Turning the roan toward the winner's circle, Ashleigh blew Samantha a kiss, then reached down to pat Shining's neck, obviously praising her amazing performance.

Looking at Tor and Mandy, Samantha said, "That's a horse who has lived up to her name. She's truly Shining now, and she will be from here on out." At their happy nods, Samantha turned to head down to the winner's circle. She had a champion to congratulate.

And somehow she knew, without a doubt, that this was just the first victory of many.